Children of Lir

STORIES FROM IRELAND

by

DESMOND HOGAN

GEORGE BRAZILLER
NEW YORK

Some of the stories in this collection first appeared in the following publications: 'The Mourning Thief' in the *New Statesman*, December 1979; 'The Man From Korea' in *Bananas*, August 1980; 'The Sojourner' in *Time Out*, October 1980; 'Soho Square Gardens' in *Green River Review*, December 1980; 'Memories of Swinging London' in *Adam International*, autumn 1979; 'Protestant Boy' in the *Literary Review*, March 1980; and 'Southern Birds' in *Granta*, December 1980

The two verses from *Red Roses for Me* by Sean O'Casey are printed by permission of Macmillan Publishers Ltd., London and Basingstoke

Published in the United States in 1981 by George Braziller, Inc.
Originally published in Great Britain 1981
by Hamish Hamilton Ltd.
Garden House 57-59 Long Acre London WC2E 9JZ

For information address the publisher:
George Braziller, Inc.
One Park Avenue, New York, NY 10016

Library of Congress Cataloging in Publication Data
    Hogan, Desmond.
        Children of Lir.

        Contents: The Mourning Thief — The Man From Korea—

    The Sojourner — (etc.)
        1. Ireland—Fiction.   I.   Title.
    PR6058.0346C48   823'.914   81-3820
    ISBN 0-8076-1015-1   AACR2

Printed in the United States of America
First Edition

In memory of my father

Contents

A sober black shawl hides her body entirely,
Touched by the sun and th' salt spray of th' sea;
But down in the darkness a slim hand so lovely,
Carries a rich bunch of red roses for me.

Sean O'Casey, Red Roses for Me

The Mourning Thief

Coming through the black night he wondered what lay
before him: a father lying dying; Christmas; midnight
ceremonies in a church which stood up like a gravestone;
floods about his home.

With him were his wife and his friend Gerard. They
needn't have come by boat but something purgatorial
demanded it of Liam, the gulls that shot over like stars, the
roxy music in the juke box, the occasional Irish ballad rising
in cherished defiance of the sea.

The night was soft, breezes intruded, plucking hair,
threads lying loose in many coloured jerseys. Susan fell
asleep once while Liam looked at Gerard. It was Gerard's
first time in Ireland; Gerard's eyes were chestnut. His dark
hair cropped like a monk's on a bottle of English brandy.
With his wife sleeping Liam could acknowledge the physical
relationship that lay between them. It wasn't that Susan
didn't know but despite the truism of promiscuity in the
school where they worked there still abided laws like the Old
Testament God's, reserving carnality for smiles after dark.

A train to Galway, the Midlands frozen in.

Susan looked out like a Botticelli Venus, a little worried,
often just vacuous. She was a music teacher, thus her mind
was penetrated by the vibrations of Bach whether in a public
lavatory or a Lyon's café.

The red house at the end of the street; it looked cold,
pushed away from the other houses. A river in flood lay
behind. A woman, his mother, greeted him. He an only

1

child, she soon to be widow. But something disturbed Liam with excitement. Christmas candles still burned in this town.

His father lay in bed, still magically alive, white hair smeared on him like a dummy, that hard face that never forgave an enemy in the police force still on him. He was delighted to see Liam. At eighty-three he was a most ancient father, marrying late, begetting late, his wife fifteen years younger.

A train brushed the distance outside. Adolescence returned with a sudden start: the gold flurry of snow as the train in which he was travelling sped towards Dublin, the films about Russian winters. Irish winters became Russian winters in turn, and half Liam's memories of adolescence were of the fantasised presence of Russia. Ikons, candles, streets agleam with snow.

'Still painting?'

'Still painting.' As though he could ever give it up. His father smiled as though he were about to grin. 'Well we never made a policeman out of you.'

At ten, the day before he was to be inaugurated as a boy scout, Liam handed in his uniform. He always hated the colours of the Irish flag, mixing like the yolk in a bad egg.

It hadn't disappointed his father that he hadn't turned into a military man, but his father preferred to hold on to a shred of prejudice against Liam's chosen profession, leaving momentarily aside one of his most cherished memories, visiting the National Gallery in Dublin once with his son, encountering the curator by accident, and having the curator show them around, an old man who'd since died, leaving behind a batch of poems and a highly publicised relationship with an international writer. But the sorest point, the point now neither would mention, was arguments about violence. At seventeen Liam walked the local hurling pitch with petitions against the war in Vietnam.

Liam's father's fame, apart from being a police inspector of note, was fighting in the GPO in 1916 and subsequently

2

being arrested on the republican side in the civil war. Liam was against violence, pure and simple. Nothing could convince him that 1916 was right. Nothing could convince him it was different from now, old women, young children, being blown to bits in Belfast.

Statues abounded in this house; in every nook and cranny was a statue, a statue of Mary, a statue of Joseph, an emblem perhaps of some saint Mrs. Fogarthy had sweetly long forgotten. This was the first thing Gerard noticed and Susan, who had seen this menagerie before, was still surprised. 'It's like a holy statue farm.'

Gerard said it was like a holy statue museum. They were sitting by the fire, two days before Christmas. Mrs. Fogarthy had gone to bed.

'It is a museum,' Liam said, 'all kinds of memories, curious sensations here, ghosts. The ghosts of Irish Republicans, of policemen, military men, priests, the ghosts of Ireland.'

'Why ghosts?' Gerard asked.

'Because Ireland is dying,' Liam said.

Just then they heard his father cough.

Mr. Fogarthy was slowly dying, cancer welling up in him. He was dying painfully and yet peacefully because he had a dedicated wife to look after him, and a river in flood around, somehow calling Christ to mind, calling penance to mind, instilling a sense of winter in him that went back a long time, a river in flood around a limestone town.

Liam offered to cook the Christmas dinner but his mother scoffed him. He was a good cook Susan vouched. Once Liam had cooked and his father had said he wouldn't give it to the dogs.

They walked, Liam, Susan, Gerard, in a town where women were hugged into coats like brown paper accidentally blown about them. They walked in the grounds of Liam's former school, once a Georgian estate, now beautiful, elegant still in the east Galway winter solstice.

3

There were tinkers to be seen in the town and English hippies behaving like tinkers. Many turkeys were displayed, fatter than ever, festooned by holly. Altogether one would notice prosperity everywhere, cars, shining clothes, modern fronts replacing the antique ones Liam recalled and pieced together from childhood.

But he would not forfeit England for this dull patch of Ireland, southern England where he'd lived since he was twenty-two; Sussex, the trees plump as ripe pears, the rolling verdure, the odd delight of an Elizabethan cottage.

He taught with Susan, with Gerard, in a free school. He taught children to paint. Susan taught them to play musical instruments. Gerard looked after younger children though he himself played a musical instrument, a cello.

Once Liam and Susan had journeyed to London to hear him play at St. Martin-in-the-Fields, entertaining ladies who wore poppies on their lapels, as his recital coincided with Remembrance Sunday and paper poppies generated an explosion of remembrance.

Susan went to bed early now, complaining of fatigue, and Gerard and Liam were left with one another. Though both were obviously male they were lovers, lovers in a tentative kind of way, occasionally sleeping with one another. It was still an experiment, but for Liam held a matrix of adolescent fantasy. Though he married at twenty-two, his sexual fantasy from adolescence was always homosexual. Susan could not complain. In fact it rather charmed her. She'd had more lovers since they'd married than fingers could count; Liam would always accost her with questions about their physicality, were they more satisfying than him? But he knew he could count on her; tenderness between them had lasted six years now.

She was English, very much English. Gerard was English. Liam was left with this odd quarrel of Irishness. Memories of adolescence at boarding school, waking from horrific dreams nightly when he went to the window to throw

4

himself out but couldn't because the window frames were jammed. His father had placed him at boarding school, to toughen him like meat. Liam had not been toughened, chastened, ran away once or twice. At eighteen he left altogether, went to England, worked on a building site, put himself through college. He'd ended up in Sussex, losing a major part of his Irishness but retaining this: a knowledge when the weather was going to change, a premonition of all kinds of disasters and, ironically, an acceptance of the worst disasters of all, death, estrangement.

Now that his father was near death old teachers, soldiers, policemen called, downing sherries, laughing rhetorically, sitting beside the bed covered by a quilt that looked like twenty inflated balloons. Sometimes Liam, Susan, Gerard sat with these people, exchanging remarks about the weather, the fringe of politics or the world economic state generally.

Mrs. Fogarthy swept up a lot. She dusted and danced around with a cloth as though she'd been doing this all her life, fretting and fiddling with the house.

Cars went by. Geese went by, clanking terribly. Rain came and church bells sounded from a disparate steeple.

Liam's father reminisced about 1916, recalling little incidents, fights with British soldiers, comrades dying in his arms, ladies fainting from hunger, escape to Mayo, later imprisonment in the Curragh during the civil war. Liam said: 'Do you ever connect it with now, men, women, children being blown up, the La Mon hotel bombing, Bessbrook killings, Birmingham, Bloody Friday? Do you ever think that the legends and the brilliance built from your revolution created this, death justified for death's sake, the stories in the classroom, the priests' stories, this language, this celebration of blood?'

Although Liam's father fought himself once he belonged to those who deplored the present violence, seeing no connection. Liam saw the connection but disavowed both.

5

'Hooligans. Murderers,' Liam's father said.

Liam said, 'You were once a hooligan then.'

'We fought to set a majority free.'

'And created the spirit of violence in the new state. We were weaned on violence, me and others of my age. Not actual violence but always with a reference to violence. Violence was right we were told in class. How can one blame those now who go out and plant bombs to kill old women when they were once told this was right.'

The dying man became angry. He didn't look at Liam, looked beyond him to the street.

'The men who fought in 1916 were heroes. Those who lay bombs in cafés are scum.'

Betrayed he was silent then, silent because his son accused him on his deathbed of unjustifiably resorting to bloodshed once. Now guns went off daily in the far off North. Where was the line between right and wrong? Who could say? An old man on his deathbed prayed that the guns he'd fired in 1916 had been for a right cause and, in the words of his leader Patrick Pearse, had not caused undue bloodshed.

On Christmas Eve the three young people and Mrs. Fogarthy went to midnight mass in the local church. In fact it wasn't to the main church but a smaller one, situated on the outskirts of the town, protruding like a headstone. A bald middle-aged priest greeted a packed congregation. The cemetery lay nearby but one was unaware of it. Christmas candles and Christmas trees glowed in bungalows.

'Come all ye faithful' a choir of matchstick boys sang. Their dress was scarlet, scarlet of joy.

Afterwards Mrs. Fogarthy penetrated the crib with a whisper of prayer.

Christmas morning, clean, spare, Liam was aware of estrangement from his father, that his father was ruminating on his words about violence, wondering were he and his ilk, the teachers, police, clergy of Ireland responsible for what was happening now, in the first place by nurturing the cult of violence, contributing to the actuality of it as expressed by young men in Belfast and London.

Sitting up on Christmas morning Mr. Fogarthy stared ahead. There was a curiosity about his forehead. Was he guilty? Were those in high places guilty as his son said?

Christmas dinner; Gerard joked, Susan smiled, Mrs. Fogarthy had a sheaf of joy. Liam tidied and somehow sherry elicited a chuckle and a song from Mrs. Fogarthy. 'I have seen the lark soar high at morn.'

The song rose to the bedroom where her husband who'd had dinner in bed heard it.

The street outside was bare.

Gerard fetched a guitar and brought all to completion, Christmas, birth, festive eating, by a rendition of Bach's 'Jesu, Joy of Man's Desiring'.

Liam brought tea to his father. His father looked at him.

''Twas lovely music,' his father said with a sudden brogue. 'There was a Miss Hanratty who lived here before you were born who studied music in Heidelberg and could play Schumann in such a way as to bring tears to the cat's eyes. Poor soul, she died young, a member of the ladies' confraternity. Schumann was her favourite and Mendelssohn came after that. She played at our wedding, your mother's and mine. She played Mozart and afterwards in the hotel sang a song, what was it? O yes, "The Star of the County Down".

'Such a sweetness she had in her voice too. But she was a bit of a loner and a bit lost here. Never too well really, she died maybe when you were a young lad.'

Reminiscences, names from the past, Catholic names, Protestant names, the names of boys in the rugby club, in the golf club, Protestant girls he'd danced with, nights at the October fair. They came easily now, a simple jargon.

Sometimes though the old man visibly stopped to consider his child's rebuke.

Liam gauged the sadness, wished he hadn't said anything,

7

wanted to simplify it but knew it possessed all the simplicity it could have, a man on his deathbed in dreadful doubt.

Christmas night they visited the convent crib, Liam, Susan, Gerard, Mrs. Fogarthy, a place glowing with a red lamp. Outside trees stood in silence, a mist thinking of enveloping them. The town lay in silence. At odd intervals one heard the gurgle of television but otherwise it could have been childhood, the fair Green, space, emptiness, the rythmn, the dance of one's childhood dreams.

Liam spoke to his father that evening. 'Where I work we try to educate children differently from other places, teach them to develop and grow from within, try to direct them from the most natural point within them. There are many such schools now but ours, ours I think is special, run as a co-operative, we try to take children from all class backgrounds and begin at the beginning to redefine education.'

'And do you honestly think they'll be better educated children than you were, that the way we educated you was wrong?'

Liam paused.

'Well it's an alternative.'

His father didn't respond, thinking of nationalistic comradely Irish school-teachers long ago. Nothing could convince him that the discipline of the old style of education wasn't better, grounding children in basic skills. Silence somehow interrupted a conversation, darkness deep around them, the water of the floods shining, reflecting stars.

Liam said goodnight. Liam's father grunted. Susan already lay in bed. Liam got in beside her. They heard a bird let out a scream in the sky like a baby and they went to sleep.

Gerard woke them in the morning, strumming a guitar.

Saint Stephen's day; mummers stalked the street, children with blackened faces in a regalia of rags collecting for the wren. Music of a tin whistle came from a pub, the town coming to life. The river shone with sun.

Susan divined a child dressed like old King Cole, a crown

8

on her head and her face blackened. Gerard was intrigued. They walked the town. Mrs. Fogarthy had lunch ready. But Liam was worried, deeply worried. His father lay above, immersed in the past.

Liam had his past too, always anxious in adolescence, running away to Dublin, eventually running away to England. The first times home had been odd; he noticed the solitariness of his parents. They'd needed him like they needed an ill-tended dog. Susan and he had married in the local church. There'd been a contagion of aunts and uncles at the wedding. Mrs. Fogarthy had prepared a meal. Salad and cake. The river had not been in flood then.

In England he worked hard. Ireland could so easily be forgotten with the imprint of things creative, children's drawings, oak trees in blossom, Tudor cottages where young women in pinafores served tea and cakes, home-made and juiced with icing.

He'd had no children. But Gerard now was both a twin, a child, a lover to him. There were all kinds of possibilities. Experiment was only beginning. Yet Ireland, Christmas, returned him to something, least of all the presence of death, more a proximity to the prom, empty laburnum pods and hawthorn trees naked and crouched with winter. Here he was at home with thoughts, thoughts of himself, of adolescence. Here he made his own being like a doll on a miniature globe. He knew whence he came and if he wasn't sure where he was going at least he wasn't distraught about it.

They walked with his mother that afternoon. Later an aunt came, preened for Christmas and the imminence of death. She enjoyed the tea, the knowledgeable silences, looked at Susan as though she was not from England but a far off country, an Eastern country hidden in the mountains. Liam's father spoke to her not of 1916 but of policemen they'd known, irascible characters, forgetting that he had been the most irascible of all, a domineering man with a wizened face ordering his inferiors around.

9

He'd brought law, he'd brought order to the town. But he'd failed to bring trust. Maybe that's why his son had left. Maybe that's why he was pondering the fate of the Irish revolution now, men with high foreheads who'd shaped the fate of the Irish Republic. His thoughts brought him to killings now being done in the name of Ireland. There his thoughts floundered.

From where arose this language of violence for the sake and convenience of violence?

Liam strode by the prom alone that evening, locked in a donkey jacket. There were rings of light around distant electric poles. He knew his father to be sitting up in bed; the policemen he'd been talking about earlier gone from his mind and his thoughts on 1916, on guns, and blazes, and rumination in prison cells long ago. And long after that thoughts on the glorification of acts of violence, the minds of children caressed with the deeds of violence. He'd be thinking of his son who fled and left the country.

His son now was thinking of the times he'd run away to Dublin, to the neon lights slitting the night, of the time he went to the river to throw himself in and didn't, of his final flight from Ireland. He wanted to say something, urge a statement to birth that would unite father and son but couldn't think of anything to say. He stopped by a tree and looked to the river. An odd car went by towards Dublin.

Why this need to run? Even as he was thinking that a saying of his father returned, 'Idleness is the thief of time.' That statement had been flayed upon him as a child, but with time, as he lived in England among fields of oak trees, that statement had changed; time itself had become the culprit, the thief. And the image of time as a thief was for ever embroiled in a particular ikon of his father's, that of a pacifist who ran through Dublin helping the wounded in 1916, was arrested, shot dead with a deaf and dumb youth. And that man, more than anybody, was Liam's hero, an

10

Irish pacifist, a pacifist born of his father's revolution, a pacifist born of his father's state.

He returned home quickly, drew the door on his father. He sat down.

'Remember, Daddy, the story you told me about the pacifist shot dead in 1916 with a deaf and dumb youth, the man whose wife was a feminist.'

'Yes.'

'Well, I was just thinking that he's the sort of man we need now, one who comes from a revolution but understands it in a different way, a creative way, who understands that change isn't born from violence but intense and self-sacrificing acts.' His father understood what he was saying, that there was a remnant of 1916 that was relevant and urgent now, that there had been at least one man among the men of 1916 who could speak to the present generation and show them that guns were not diamonds, that blood was precious, that birth most poignantly issues from restraint.

Liam went to bed. In the middle of the night he woke muttering to himself 'May God have mercy on your soul', although his father was not yet dead, but he wasn't asking God to have mercy on his father's soul but on the soul of Ireland, the many souls born out of his father's statelet, the women never pregnant, the cruel and violent priests, the young exiles, the old exiles, those who could never come back.

He got up, walked down the stairs, opened the door on his father's room. Inside his father lay. He wanted to see this with his own eyes, hope even in the persuasion of death.

He returned to bed.

His wife turned away from him but curiously that did not hurt him because he was thinking of the water rising, the moon on the water and as he thought of these things geese clanked over, throwing their reflections onto the water grazed with moon which rimmed this town, the church towers, the slate roofs, those that slept now, those who didn't remember.

11

The Man from Korea

Afterwards it had the awkward grace of a legend; a silence when his name was mentioned, an implied understanding of what had happened. Few know what actually happened though, so to make it easier for you to understand I will make my own version.

I was five when he came to town, a child at street corners. I was an intensely curious child, a seer, one who poked into everyone's houses and recalled scandal, chagrin and disgrace. I know all about the Hennessys and if I don't let me pretend to.

He came in 1956. He was a young man of twenty-nine but already there was something old about him. He recalled the fires of the Korean war. He'd been an American pilot there. I'm not sure what he saw but it left his face with a curious neglect of reality; he stared ahead. Sometimes a donkey, a flying piece of hay, a budding tree at the end of the street would enthral him but otherwise silence. He kept quiet. He kept his distance. He shared very few things but he talked much to me. By a fire in the Hennessys', flames spitting and crying out, he talked of the sacred places of Asia, shrines to draconian goddesses, seated statues of Buddah.

I always nodded with understanding.

I suppose that's why he trusted me. Because, although a child of five, I was used to lengthy conversations with fire brigade men, painters, road sweepers. So he and I discussed Buddah, Korea and sunsets which made you forget war, long raving sunsets, sunsets of ruby and a red brushed but not destroyed by orange. The air became red for odd moments in Korea; the redness stood in the air, so much so you could almost ensnare a colour.

He had blond hair, sharpened by glints of silver and gold, a face tainted by a purple colour. It was as though someone had painted him, brush strokes running through his appearance, a glow, a healthiness about it, yet always a malign image before his eyes that kept him quiet, that compelled an austerity into eyes that would otherwise have been lit by handsomeness in the middle of a strange, arresting and, for an Irish small town, very distinctive face.

He came in April, time when the hedgerows were blossoming, time when tinkers moved on and anglers serenely stood above the river. Light rains penetrated his arrival; talk of fat trout and drone of drovers in the pub next door to the Hennessys in the evening.

The Hennessys were the most auspicious young ladies in town. Margaret and Mona. They'd been left a small fortune by a father who won the Irish Sweep Stakes once and the pools another time. Their father had spent his whole life gambling. His wife had left him in the middle of it all. But before he died he won large stakes of money and these passed to his daughters. So his life wasn't in vain. They made sure of that, gambling and feasting themselves, an accordion moving through the night, taking all into its rhythms, sound of a train, flash of a bicycle light. The Hennessy girls sported and sang, inflaming passions of spinsters, rousing priests like devils, but retaining this in their sitting room, a knowledge of joy, a disposition for good music and songs that weren't loud and sluttish but graced by magic. Such were the songs I heard from bed up the road, songs about the Irish heart for ever misplaced and wandering on Broadway or in Sydney, Australia, miles from home, but sure of this, its heritage of bog, lake and Irish motherhood.

The Hennessys had no mother; she'd gone early but their house was opened as a guest-house before their father won

13

his fortunes and so it continued, despite money and all, less a guest-house, more a hospice for British anglers and Irish circus artistes. One travelling painter with a circus painted the Rock of Cashel on the wall. A fire blazed continually in the back room and the sweetness of hawthorn reigned.

You don't bring hawthorn into the house; it's bad luck, but the Hennessys had no mind for superstition and their house smelt of hedgerow, was smitten by sound of distant train, and warmed by a turf fire. Karl came to this house in 1956.

He meant to stay for a few weeks. His stay lasted the summer and if he did go early in autumn it was only because there was hurt in his stay.

The girls at first kept their distance, served him hot tea, brown bread, Chivers marmalade. He spent a lot of time by the fire, not just staring into it but regulating his thoughts to the outbursts of flame. He had seen war and one was aware of that; he was making a composition from war, images of children mowed down and buildings in flame. He came from a far country and had been in another far country. He was a stranger, an ex-soldier, but he was capable of recognising the images of the world he hailed from in the flames of a fire in a small town in Ireland. I suppose that's why people liked him. He had the touch, just the touch of a poet.

Margaret and Mona nursed him like a patient; making gestures towards his solitude, never venturing too far but the tone of their house altering; the parties easing out and a meditativeness coming, two girls staring into a fire, recalling their lives.

Their father had brought them up, a man in a coffee coloured suit, white shirt always open. They'd been pretty girls with ribbons like banners on their heads. Their father would bring them to the bog, bring them on picnics by the river, bring them on outings to Galway. Not a very rich man, he was rent collector, but eventually won all around him and left them wealthy.

14

Karl when he came sat alone a lot, walked the limestone streets, strolled by the river. His shirt, like their father's, was white and open necked, his suit when he wore it granite grey but more than often he wore jeans and shirts, dragon red with squares of black on them.

Even his eyebrows were blond, coming to a sudden quizzical halt.

He often smoked a cigarette as though it was a burden. Sometimes a bird seemed to shock him or a fish leaping with a little quiver of jubilation. The mayfly came, the continual trespass of another life on the water.

I followed Karl, the stranger, watched him sit by the river, close to the sign advertising God. 'What shall it profit a man; if he shall gain the whole world, and lose his own soul?'

An elm tree sprayed with life in a field. A young man sat on the grass by the river. The Elizabethan fortress shouldered ivy.

Karl spoke little and when he did it was in the evening, in the pub, to the drovers. He was 'The Yank', but people tolerated this in him. He had no big car, no fast money, an urgency in his quietness, a distinction in his brows.

Margaret and Mona accustomed themselves to him and brought him to the bog with them. On an old ass and cart. Two young ladies with pitch forks in the bog, bottles of orange juice readily available, plastic bags of ice, and the summer sun at its height above them, grazing their work with its heat, its passing shadows, its sweltering fog towards evening. He helped them, becoming tanned; the complexion of sand on him, in his face, above his eyes, in his hair. He worked hard and silently. The ass wandered by the river and the girls frequently assessed the situation, sitting, drinking orange.

Margaret was the youngest but looked older; tall, pinched, cheek bones like forks on her and eyes that shot out, often venomously, often of an accord of their own, chestnut eyes that flashed and darted about and told an uncertain tale.

15

Mona was softer, younger looking, mouse hair on her, a bush of it and eyes that were at once angelic and reasonable. Her eyes told no tales though.

The river running through the bog was a savage one, foraging and digging, a merciless river that took sharp corners. Donkeys lazed by it; cows explored it; reeds shot up in it; in summer a silver glow on it that seduced.

Margaret and Mona were tolerant of me, using me to do messages, paying me with goldgrain biscuits or pennies. I talked to them though they didn't listen. They made a lot of cakes now and I sat, licking bowls. Karl received their attention with moderate ease. He was slightly afraid of it yet glad of their kindness.

I felt him to be gentle though I wouldn't go so far as to say he hadn't done terrible things; however, what was more than likely was that he was haunted by the deeds of others.

In mid July an American aunt came and visited Margaret and Mona, a lady from Chicago. She was from Karl's city and Karl visibly recoiled, going out more, seeking bog and river. This lady danced around; trimmed her eyebrows a lot; polished her nails.

She kept the girls in abeyance, talked to them as though talking to pet dogs. She had a blue hat that leapt up with a start, a slight veil hanging from the hat. She challenged everyone, me included, as to who they were, where they were from, who their parents were and what their ambition in life was. Karl was unforthcoming. I told her I was going to be a fire brigade man in China, but Karl said nothing, pulled on a cigarette, his eyes lifting a little.

She wanted to know where in Chicago he hailed from. He muttered something and she chattered on again, encompassing many subjects in her discursiveness, talking about the weather, the bog, her relatives in Armagh, Chicago, the Great Lakes, golf, swimming, croquet, timber forests, Indian reservations, the Queen, Prince Philip and lastly her

16

dog who'd jumped under a car one day when he'd been feeling – understandably – despairing.

Karl looked as though he was about to go when she left. The girls moved closer then, tried to ruffle him a bit, demanded more of him. He sang songs for them, recited poetry about American Indians. They listened. Mona had a song or two, songs about death and the banshee's call to death. Margaret was jealous of Mona's voice and showed her jealousy by pursing her scarlet lips.

They had parties again, entertaining the roguish young clerks. They had dances and sing-songs, the gramophone searing the nights with Ginger Rogers.

Karl went to church with them sometimes. He looked at the ceremonies as though at something difficult to understand, the hurried Latin, the sermons by the priest always muttered so low no one could hear them.

Mona went to Dublin early in September and bought new clothes. Margaret followed her example in doing this.

I went into the sitting room one evening and Margaret had her arm on Karl's shoulder. He talked about the war now for the first time, the planes, the screams, trees and houses fighting for their lives, the children moaning and the women grabbing their children. He recalled the fighter planes, the village targets; he spoke of the mercilessness of war. People asked for alms. They got war. Margaret recounted her father's tales about the Black and Tans, the butcheries, the maiming, and Mona philosophically added, 'Thank God we didn't have Churchill or Hitler here. Those men were just interested in the money.'

Margaret chirped in: 'About time someone got interested in money. They're starving beyond in England and Germany for want of money. We're lucky here.'

Ireland was the land of full and plenty to them, legends about other countries somehow awry.

Margaret boldly got up, put on the gramophone while I was there one evening and asked Karl to dance. Whereupon

17

he threw off his shoes and danced with her, a waltz, the kernel of the music binding them together.

Mona watched, quiet but not too jealous. They'd always been strange together and now the strangeness emerged. They saw in Karl a common ideal. They wanted to get him come Hell or high water. High water came with the floods in early October. Mona outshone herself, russet in her hair, a dress of lilac and her arms brown from summer. Margaret became pertinent to the fact that Mona was more attractive than she so she did many things, wore necklaces of pearl, daubed her lips in many colours, wore even higher high heels. She stood above Mona and was nearly as tall as Karl.

Their house had a bad reputation and now Margaret began appearing like an expensive courtesan; she wore her grandmother's fur to the pictures while all the time Mona shone with the grace of a Michaelmas daisy.

Geese clanked over; bare trees were reflected in water. The sun was still warm, the vibrancy and health of honey in it. The leaves had fallen prematurely and the floods had arrived before their time but still the days were warm and Mona wore sandals while Karl sported light jackets.

The ladies of town noted the combat between the two girls, or rather Margaret's unusual assertiveness. They were overjoyed and sensed a coming downfall on a house which had distressed them so much with its joyful sounds.

Karl had taken to talking to me, talking about Korea, Chicago, war, the race problem. He found a unique audience in me and I listened to everything and I watched his silences, his playing cards by himself. I started accompanying him on his walks; he sometimes sitting to read Chinese poems out loud while cows mooed appreciatively.

He took my hand once or twice and distilled in me the sense of a father. I suppose with Karl holding my hand then I decided I would have a child of my own some day, a male child.

Karl spoke, spoke of the weather in Chicago, winter

18

storms over the Great Lakes, ice skating, swimming in the huge oblong winter pools. There was something Chicago didn't yield him though despite multi-layered ice-creams or skyscrapers always disappearing into the clouds, and that was the sky of Ireland, clouds over the mustard-coloured marshes, Atlantic clouds heaving and blowing and provoking rancour in the bog water. He'd come to our town looking for the ease of an Eastern shrine, found it. Now two young women were vying for him.

He spoke about his mother, his father, Americans, scoffed at the American belief in war. I told my parents that Karl didn't believe in war and they didn't hear me. I told my grandfather. Eventually I told our dog.

To the women of town Margaret and Mona were as courtesans, they'd stopped going to mass. God knows what they were doing with that American.

They made cakes, desserts, cups of tea for him. Eventually he tired of their intricacies and reached for them. One evening I came in the front door, pulled back the curtain to see Karl with Mona in his arms, her dress at her waist, her breasts heaving in her bra. I sped off.

I returned some evenings later, peeping through the curtains to find Margaret in a similar position.

Then one evening I came and the lights were off except for one red bulb that Karl had inserted. He and Mona were dancing to music from the radio in semi-darkness, the fire splurting and a rose light overlooking them, holding them.

This time I waited. I watched through the curtains as they danced, Karl reaching to kiss Mona. Their kiss was tantalizing. He removed her ribbon. Hair shot out like a hedgehog's prickles.

I knew Margaret to be in Dublin. I watched them leave the room. He following her. I looked at Our Lady on an altar and she looked back at me quizzically. Outside a cat protested.

I don't know what happened that evening. I always

imagine Margaret returned prematurely from Dublin and found them sleeping. But Karl left without saying goodbye and of all hurts I've had in my life that remains the most instant, the first hurt of life. My father, brother, friend didn't acknowledge that a farewell was necessary.

It doesn't seem like a major incident looking back, but it took the rainbow from the girls' eyes, the flush from their cheeks, the splendour from their dress. Jealousy created a barrier. It created an iron curtain. Jealousy came and sat where Karl had once sat. Jealousy came, another tenuous stranger.

He was a celibate and didn't wish to make love to either but took Mona as an off-chance and showed to Margaret all that was missing in her, real physical beauty, a good singing voice.

Mona under the weight of Margaret's acrimony became plump, looked like an orphan in the convent.

No more parties, no more songs; many guests, much work.

And then in spring Mona left on the evening train. I went to the station with Margaret to say goodbye to her. Margaret looked like a lizard, fretful. Mona was wrapped like a Hungarian refugee. The sisters didn't kiss but I can still see the look in Mona's eyes. She'd been betrayed by Margaret's loss of faith in her. She undid her own beauty, the beauty of her soul as well as the beauty of her body to satisfy an impatient sister.

Years later when Mona was dying of cancer in a Birmingham hospital Margaret visited her. There was still no forgiveness, but both of them had forgotten what it was exactly which had come between them; a burgeoning of possibilities in the form of a young ex-soldier, an eye to another world. I doubt if either of them ever for a moment reached that other world but they were left with an intuition of it long after their father's money had run out.

Mona died a few years ago.

20

Margaret still runs the guest-house. And me? - I put these elements together to indicate their existence, that of Margaret and Mona, their enchantment with a young man who came and unnerved us all and left a strange aftermath, way back there in childhood, a shadow on the water, the cry of a wild goose in pain, an image of tranquillity in far off Asia where candles burned before perennial gods, gods untouched by war, by the search of a young man, by the iniquitous failure of two young women who reached and whose fingers failed to grasp.

The Sojourner

He lived in a little room in Shepherd's Bush. There was a bed for himself and above a little compartment for visitors. One climbed by ladder to this area. A curtain separated it from the rest of the room. It was this area he'd reserved for Moira.

Around the walls were accumulated Italian masterpieces, pieces of Titian, pieces of Tintoretto, arms by Caravaggio, golden and brusque. Dominating all was a Medici face by Botticelli. Above the fireplace a young man, stern, glassy eyed, his lips satisfied, his stare resigned to the darkness of the room, a darkness penetrated by the light of one window.

Jackie worked on a building site. He'd worked on one since he'd come over in February. Previously he'd been a chef in a café in Killarney, riding to and from work on a motorbike. But something made him go, family problems, spring, lust.

The room had been conveniently vacated by two Provisional Sinn Fein members from Kerry. He'd scraped Patrick Pearse from the wall. They were gone to another flat.

He'd risen early on mornings when Shepherd's Bush had been suffocated in cold white fog, a boy from Ireland hugging himself into a donkey jacket. He'd been picked up in a lorry, driven to diverse sites. Now the mornings were warm. Blue crept along the corners of high rise flats, lingering bits of dawn. Jackie was enclosed in a routine, last night's litter outside country and western pubs, Guinness bottles, condoms, the refuse of Ireland in exile. The work was hard but then there was Moira to think of. At odd moments when life was harsh or reality pressing her image veered towards him; as he sat in the lorry, tightening his fists in the pockets of his donkey jacket, as he sat over a mug of tea in the site office. Moira Finnerty was his sister, at present in a mental hospital in Limerick but shortly to be released. She was coming to London to stay with him.

Jackie and Moira had grown up on a lowly farm in the Kerry mountains. Their parents had been quiet, gruff, physically in love with one another until their sixties. A grandfather lived with them, always telling indecent stories. There'd been many geese, cows, a mare always looking in the direction of the ocean, a blizzard of gulls always blowing over the fields. Life had been hard. Jackie had gone to school in Killarney. Moira had attended a convent in Cahirciveen.

Jackie had peddled dope at fifteen in the juke box cafés of Killarney. His first affair had been at sixteen with the daughter of a rich American business man, sent to the convent in Killarney by way of a quirk. After all Killarney was prettier than Lucerne or Locarno and it was possessed of its own international community. Sarah was from Michigan, randy, blonde, fulsome. She'd always had money, a plethora of nuns chasing her. However she'd avoided the nuns, sat in jeans, which always looked as though they were about to explode, in cafés, smoking French cigarettes, smattering the air with French fumes.

Sex for Jackie until now was associated with the sea; recalling Sarah he thought more of an intimacy with the sea, with beaches near Ballinskelligs, inlets with the spire of Skellig Mhicel in the distance, an odd mound in the sea where monks once sang Deus Meus, the chants of Gaelic Ireland before Elizabethan soldiers sailed westwards on currachs.

Sarah had gone. There'd been many girls, Killarney was full of girls. He did his Leaving Certificate twice which led to nights lounging in cafés in Killarney, Valentine cards circulating from year to year, and one ice-cream parlour in

23

Killarney where a picture of a Spanish poet stood alongside pictures of Powerscourt House, County Wicklow, and Ladies' View, Killarney, one tear dropping out of his eye, rolling up in a little quizzical ball and a bullet wound in his head. It was an odd cartoon to show in a café but then the owners were Portuguese so one accepted the odd divergence more easily.

Jackie had gone to Dublin, worked on building sites, peddled dope; lived like a prince in Rathmines. However, the arm of the law fell upon him. He was imprisoned for six months, returned to Kerry. A good cook, he got a job in a café in a world of provincial Irish cafés, always the juke-box pounding out the bleeding heart of provincial Ireland, songs about long distance lorry drivers and tragic deaths in Kentucky.

His sister emerged from convent school about this time, got a job in a hospital in Limerick. It was supposed to be temporary but she stayed there. Moira, when she hadn't been at school, had spent her adolescence wandering the hills about their home. There'd been few trees so one could always pick her out. She'd rarely gone to dances and when she had she'd always left early before the other girls, thumbing home.

They rarely spoke, but there was always something there, a mirror-like silence. Jackie saw himself in Moira, saw the inarticulate disparate things, a moment of high on an acid trip in Rathmines, a moment of love in a café in Killarney, a moment of reverie by the sea in Ballinskelligs. The West of Ireland for all its confusion was full of these things and it was these people Jackie veered towards, people who spoke a secret language like the tinkers' Shelta.

You discerned sensitivity in people or you didn't. Jackie was an emotional snob. He was a snob in clothes, in cigarettes, in brands of dope even. But one thing he never minded was working and mending his way among the semi-literate.

24

Moira had spent two years in Limerick when she had an affair with an older married man. The usual. He made love to her, took every advantage of her shy, chubby body. Then returned to the suburbs. It was more than that which made Moira crack up. Her parents seemed content to leave her, not to expect anything remarkable of her. By solicitude they condemned her to a life of non-achievement.

Jackie had gone by the time Moira was put in the mental hospital in Limerick. Her face pressed on him. At first he thought to go back and rescue her. But he relied on time and patience. Moira was to be let out in June. He wrote and asked her to come and stay with him. For a while.

Early June in Shepherd's Bush, the young of London walked along the street. Bottles flew. Bruce Lee continually played in the cinema. Irish country and western singers roared out with increasing desperation and one sensed behind the songs about Kerry and Cavan, mothers and luxuriant shamrock, the foetus of an unborn child urging its way from the womb of a girl over for a quick abortion.

Sometimes Jackie allowed himself to be picked up. He'd long lost interest sexually in women. The last girl he'd actually wanted to make love to had been in Dublin, a blonde who ran away to a group in California, mystical and foreign to the Irish experience. Walking in Shepherd's Bush was like walking among the refuse of other people's lives, many bins in the vicinity. He read many paperbacks. On colder days he lit fires in his room and sat over them like a tinker. Above the door was a Saint Brigid's cross which traditionally kept away evil. He'd bought it at the Irish tourist office in Bond Street. There was a desk in his room on which he wrote letters home. He thought of his mother with her giant chamber pot which had emerald patterns of foliage on it. She'd bought it in an antique shop in Listowel. He thought of his father, a randy look always in his eye. As children they'd hear their parents making love like people in far off cities in a far off time were supposed to. He could still distinguish his mother's orgasms, a cry in the air, a siren which was sublimated into the sound of a gull, the sound of a train veering towards Tralee.

They'd only had one another, he and Moira. They'd made the most of it.

Now he wrote to her.

Dear Moira,
Expecting you soon. The weather is changeable here. The job's hard. I think I may go to Copenhagen in autumn. See you soon.
Love,
Jackie.

She arrived unexpectedly one morning. The doorbell exploded. He jumped up. Oddly enough he was on the upper tier. He'd gone up there for a change. He climbed down the ladder, went to the door. He'd overslept. She was there, with two cases, scarf on her head, something more moderate about her face, less of the mysticism.

They kissed. Her breath smelt of Irish mints.

As there was no coffee he made her tea which they had on the floor. He was late for work but he decided to go anyway as he was on a nearby site. She'd sleep. He'd be back later. He bid her goodbye. She lay asleep in the upper bed. Before closing the door he looked around this den of loneliness. Moira's slip lay over a chair.

She had the room tidy when he returned and she herself looked refreshed, having bathed in the grotty bath with its reverential gas-flame bursting into life. Her scent had changed. There were perfumes of two kinds of soap in it.

This time she made him tea and they sat down. He didn't want to ask her about the mental hospital so instead he queried her about home. Moira didn't want to talk about home so instead she imparted gossip about D.J.s on Irish radio.

Jackie made a meal, one he'd been preparing in his mind for a long time, lamb curry. Afterwards they had banana crumble and custard, eating on the floor. Moira said it would be necessary for her to get a job. Jackie didn't disagree. Moira read the little pieces of print stuck about. A line from Yeats. An admonition from Socrates. Soon a point came whereby there seemed nothing else to talk about so both were silent.

They went for a drink before going to bed. Jackie apologised for the grottiness of the pub. Moira said she didn't mind, her eyes drifting about to young Irish men holding their sacred pints of Guinness.

Afterwards they returned through the dustbins and slept in their individual beds.

It being summer Moira got a job in a nearby ice-cream parlour, dressing in white, doling out runny ice-cream to West Indian children. In a generally bad summer the weather suddenly brightened and Jackie was conscious of himself, a young Adonis on a building site. His body had hardened, muscle upon muscle defining themselves. His hair was short. His face more than anything was defined, those bright blue eyes that shot out, often angry without a reason as though some subconscious hurt was disturbing him.

What he resented was the young Irish students who were arriving on the building site. They brought with them a gossipy closeness to Ireland and a lack of seriousness in their separation from that country. However, he and Moira were getting on exceedingly well. There was less talk of trauma than he'd anticipated. They had drinks, meals, outings together. On Sundays there was Holland Park and Kensington Gardens. They had picnics there. Sometimes they swam in the Serpentine. Moira's head dipped a lot, into magazines, into flowers, into the grass. The vestiges of wardship were leaving. Jackie often felt like knocking back a lock of Moira's hair. Something about her invited these gestures, her total preoccupation with a Sunday newspaper cartoon, her gaze that sometimes went from you and turned inwards, to that area they both held in common.

Moira cooked sometimes. She was a plain cook but a good one. She made brown bread much like his mother's. Jackie's cooking was more prodigious, curries that always scared Moira, lest there be drugs in them, chicken paprika, beef goulash, moussaka, and then the plates of Ireland, Limerick ham glazed in honey, Dublin coddle, Irish stew.

The divisions in the room were neatly made, borders between her area and his. Both were exceptionally neat.

For the first time she mentioned the mental hospital. It slipped out. There had been a woman there who'd had nine children, whose husband had left her, who scrubbed floors in a café and who'd eventually cracked up. In a final gesture of humiliation she'd wept while mopping the floor one day so that the proprietor reckoned she should see a psychiatrist. 'Jesus, I'm crying. I'm just crying,' she'd shouted. 'I'm just crying because they told me life would be better, men helpful. I'm just crying and I'm not ashamed. I can manage. I can manage myself.' They'd told her she couldn't and quietly stole her children, placing them in homes. It was then she'd cracked up, looking like all the other mad visionary women of Ireland, women who claimed to have seen Marie Goretti in far-flung cottages.

'They force you to crack up,' Moira said, 'so that they can be satisfied with their own lot. After all the idea of pain, real pain, is too big to cope with. Pain can be so beautiful. The pain of recognising how hopeless things are yet accepting and somehow building from it.'

His sister had grown. More than that she'd become beautiful, her Peruvian eyes calm and often a scarlet ribbon in her hair. Playing a game they'd played as children both of them dressed up at nights and went to showband concerts. Whatever her other sophistications Moira had not relinquished the showband world so they traipsed off to pubs,

Moira in a summer dress, Jackie in a suit, a green silk Chinese tie on him, girls from Offaly moaning into microphones. You were scrutinized at the doors lest you were not Irish. Often there was some doubt about Jackie until he opened his mouth. Inside people jostled, a majority of women edged for a man. Lights changed from scarlet to blue and somehow Moira in her dreamy, virginal way seemed at home here, lost in a reverie of rural Ireland.

Shyness had gone, a kind of frankness prevailed. Often Jackie sat around his room in just trousers. Moira washed in her slip, sometimes it falling over her hips.

'You know we made a pact, didn't we, when we were growing up?' Jackie said one evening, 'Mammy and Daddy never seemed to notice us.'

It was true. Against their parents' carnality they'd chosen a kind of virginal complacency.

Once in Kerry, looking at the moon, Moira had stated that this country had always been a country of nuns. In ancient times nuns had built cottages by nearby beaches.

It was less that they were a nun and a monk, more that they had to resist. Resist their parents' self-absorption, resist the geese, the skies, the dun of the mountains, the purple changing to green of the rocks.

Jackie had had his affairs. In fact Moira had hers. But it was as though they'd made a vow of celibacy when Jackie was thirteen and Moira eleven; they didn't want to fall into the trap of closing themselves off. They wanted to be open, romantic, available. Looking into Moira's eyes before going to bed Jackie saw that in fact they were closing themselves off in a different way.

They were outsiders, resigned to be outsiders and were making a fetish of this role. Moira had picked up a little teddy-bear in Shepherd's Bush market. In her bed she held it. She was sitting up in her slip. 'Good-night Jackie,' she said.

The teddy-bear slept with her.

29

That night Jackie walked the environs of Shepherd's Bush, sat in a café, spoke to a man from Ghana. He waited some hours. The first light came. He returned home, picked up his things for work, waited for a lorry on Shepherd's Bush Green.

She wanted to dance now so she danced with him. They travelled to Kilburn and Camden. Saturday nights in ballrooms, the London Irish swung to visiting showbands. Despite this venture in a foreign city Moira had a lonesomeness for the decay of rural Ireland, for its fetishes. Jackie dancing with her, cheek to cheek, wondered if he could cure it.

It was a miserable summer weather-wise. Early in August there was a much advertised march against troops in Northern Ireland. Jackie and Moira saw it by accident, young English people shouting about women in Northern Ireland jails.

Later that month the Queen's cousin was blown up in County Sligo. Moira and Jackie didn't listen to the radio much but they heard a jumbled commentary on the events. Jackie wondered about the Provisional Sinn Fein people who'd lived in this room once, that was their domain, instant and shocking deaths in the cause of Ireland. He smiled. No one in the whole of London reprimanded Jackie or Moira but the papers were full of hatred, mistaking the source of the guilt.

The guilt was a shared one Jackie thought, a handed down one. Everyone's hands were dipped in blood; blood of intolerance. He'd thought about it so much, knew the kind of prevalent and often justified anger of Irish republicans. In Kerry they were eccentrics. One I.R.A. man he knew grew the best marijuana in Kerry and decorated it with Christmas decorations come Christmas. Often Northern republicans fled to his house, men with trapped eyes. Reaching to them was like reaching to dynamite. They hit back easily.

So Jackie and Moira assumed responsibility for the deaths

of the Earl Mountbatten, the Dowager Lady Brabourne and the two children killed with them. They walked about London with the air of criminals. The newspapers had ordained this guilt. Jackie and Moira accepted it, not as slaves but with a certain grandeur. They were Irish and as such bore a kind of mass guilt, guilt for the republican few, for the order of the gun, the enslaved and frightened eyes, the winsome thoughts of Patrick Pearse. It was all part of their heritage; to deny it would be like denying the wet weather. But in accepting a certain responsibility both knew, Jackie more than Moira, of a more real tradition which never met English eyes, the tradition of the great families of Kerry, the goblets of wine, the harp, the Gregorian chant.

They'd left Kerry with their wolfhounds, going to Europe, but something was always ready to be disturbed of this tradition, a hedge-schoolmaster behind a white hawthorn tree reading Cicero, O'Connell, another Kerryman, in Clontarf telling the Irish proletariat that the freedom of Ireland is not worth the shedding of one drop of blood, Michael Davitt in Clare leading a silent pacifist march against English landlords.

Jackie knew, as all sensitive and knowledgeable Irish people knew, that the prevalent philosophy of Irish history was pacifism and he could therefore accept the rebukes of the English newspapers with glee, with a certain amount of wonder, knowing them to be founded and spread in ignorance.

But Moira wasn't so sure. He'd noticed her fluctuating somewhat. Although outwardly calm there was a new intensity in her dancing. She was going back, quicker than he could cope with, to the ballroom floors in Kerry, the point at which all is surrendered, the days of drudgery, the nights of squalid sex in the backs of cars. She was trying to be peaceful with a violent heritage.

In a dancehall one night there was a fight. Someone hit

31

someone else on the head with a chair. A woman started singing 'God save Ireland said the Heroes' and in moments Jackie's dreams of pacificism were gone. A young man made a speech about H. Blocks on the counter and somewhere an auburn haired woman described her lust for a Clare farmer.

Jackie took Moira home. She began crying, sitting on a chair.

In moments it was gone, a summer of harmony. The tears came, scarlet, outraged blue. Afterwards it was the silence which was compelling. She was steadily recalling the corners of a mental hospital, the outreaches of pain. Her heart in a moment had turned to stone.

It was a curious stone too which her heart had become, exquisite and frail in its own way. She began going to dances by herself and one night she did not return. Jackie sat up, waiting until the small hours. When there was no sign of her he went out for a while, hugging himself into a donkey jacket. Autumn was coming.

People are like doctors. We live with one another for a while. We cure one another. Jackie saw himself as physician but too late. Moira no longer needed his physician's touch. She was sleeping around, compulsively giving herself, engineering all kinds of romances. And when she stopped talking to him much he too searched the night for strangers. At first unsuccessfully. But then they came, one by one, Argentinians, West Indians.

She perceived the domain of his life, said nothing.

'Pope visits war-torn country', the papers warned.

It was true, John Paul was coming, giving an ultimate benediction to the dancehalls, the showbands, the neon lights, the juke-boxes that shook jauntily with their burden of song.

He saw the look on Moira's face and knew she was destined to return. Nothing could hold her back. Dancing to an Irish showband singer's version of 'One Day at a Time' he realized her need for the hurt, the intimacy, the pain of ballroom Ireland. She wanted to be immolated by these things.

There was nothing he could say against it. It was his life against hers and she saw his life as a shambles. He couldn't tell her about the boys with diamond eyes, no more than she could tell him about the lads from Cork who jumped on her as though she was an old and unusable mattress. In mid-September she announced her decision.

A bunch of marigolds sat on the mantlepiece, a little throne of tranquillity.

'Will you come too?' she said.

'No,' he said and half-naked he looked at her. He wanted to ask her why it was necessary always to return to the point where you were rejected, but such questions were useless. The Pope was coming, the music of ballroom Ireland was strong in her ears.

He took her to Euston and she asked him if he had any messages for their parents.

'Tell them I won't be home for Christmas,' he said.

She looked at him. Her eyes looked as though they were going to pop out and grapple him and take their mutual pain but they did no such thing.

Later that night Jackie wandered on Shepherd's Bush. He knew he'd deceived himself, going from body to body, holding out hope he'd meet someone who'd fulfil some childhood dream of purity.

All his life he'd been trying to reconstruct her, not so much Moira, as that virgin of Ireland, Our Lady of Knock, Our Lady of the Sorrows, that complacent maiden who edged into juke-box cafés, into small towns where apparitions had taken place in the last century and now neon strove into the rain.

He wouldn't go to Copenhagen. He'd go south. He'd pack up his things and leave, knowing there a certain compulsion about the sun, the Mediterranean, the shine of the sun on southern beaches.

Before leaving London there was one thing he wanted to do, dress up like any other Irish boy, comb his hair, put on his green Chinese tie and dance until all was forgotten, the lights of Killarney, the whine of the juke-box, the look on Moira's face as she stared over a stone wall in Kerry, into a world which would consume their knowledge of the sea, their knowledge of stone, their reverence of one another.

Soho Square Gardens

Coming from the north early that winter entailed arriving from snow, lilac gas works, the odd ember of a sunset over a city, a tree, a dustbin. Twenty-eight, I was shattered by the death of my parents. A new life had to be found, away from the north, away from Durham, away from the convolutions of friends, the camaraderie of pubs, northern accents, clinging hands of women, half-Marxist, half monopoly capitalist, preaching workers' solidarity and reaching for all that was material. I left the place of my youth.

They'd been killed the previous winter, the very end of it, tricked by a sliver of frost on a Yorkshire road.

My father a bank manager, my mother, well, she a cook, a player of bridge, a good dresser, a hostess who wrought Irish cousins and British colonels into her pattern. They going, my Irish background went like a disappearing angel, the last touches of childhood holidays in Kerry or Cork, depending from which angle I looked, my mother's parents or my father's.

Leaving the north of England for the south I knew it wasn't a part of England, fundamentally, I was saying goodbye to but Ireland, the mysterious gales, the mysterious clouds, the world that existed behind the real world of our home, the past, the country from which my parents came, the country they could not forget.

Everything was set up for me in London, a room in Soho, contacts, introductions. I'd already been contracted to work for a nature magazine for three months. My photographs were well known. I'd exhibited in London previously. My work appeared in leading magazines. I had a darkroom in Soho now, a bed, a table, a window that looked on a street of sex shops, the odd pub, a wine shop, and a few Greek restaurants with lusty Greek women portrayed outside dancing to an orchestra of bulging Greeks and Turks.

The one thing that amazes me about photography is the way one minute you don't have anything and the next, a miracle, an image appears, a tree, a child, a gutter, something caught, something placed in this mesmeric confusion some call life, others have no name for. Photography for me is as philosophy to Heidegger, a way of approaching the unique metaphors of existence because I believe that somewhere there lies a heart, a soul, a centre. Call it God, call it what you like, I suppose it's what makes art tick over and astronomers sometimes numb, gazing into a constellation of stars which diversify and explode into music, into philosophy, into rambling questions about life, death, and after-life. Physical death, the death of parents for instance, engenders these questions. Forgive me if I sound vague. I don't mean to. I'm trying to describe how it is living when your parents are gone, your past is gone and your present is a little patch of pursuit, cameras, darkrooms, visions on celluloid of fields in Somerset, Sussex or sunsets over Soho Square Gardens.

I was living a stone's throw from the gardens, a milieu of winos, office workers, children paddling in the grass. The area had its own distinctive sex shops mingled with food reeking of Tuscany or Umbria, but the gardens above all had character and figures stood out in these gardens, hallucinations at dawn when I walked, working up enthusiasm for another day.

It was in Soho Square Gardens I met Lily.

She was talking to herself one bitterly cold morning, saying over and over again that men are shits but the worst are Irishmen. Lily was from Mayo.

I spoke to her, telling her my parents were Irish.

She was about forty-two, blonde hair dyed, margarine coloured, fragments and filters of white in it as though she might have been a circus beauty once. I asked her why men were shits and she told me that Kavanagh had just left her, a Galwayman. Two years together. He'd gone back to Galway city, heard the EEC had brought prosperity, Russian liners coming in, brothels opening and all-night restaurants where they served crab soup.

Lily was alone.

I took her home, gave her tea. Then she said she had to go to mass. Saint Patrick's in Soho. She was a middle-aged woman reawakening to Catholicism. I looked at her, eyes big as marble rocks, green in her eyes, the enduring green of Connemara marble.

She said: 'If Kavanagh is gone at least I have Saint Anthony.'

I went with her to the church where I was introduced to Saint Anthony, an uninspiring statue.

She said, 'Many's the time I was without and he heard me.' She put two pence in the collection box.

A priest droned. I told her to call again. She said she would. She lived nearby over an Italian delicatessen.

I suppose I knew by her she'd been a prostitute or was now.

She called again. One night when I was asleep. She brought Silvano with her, a boy who worked in a striptease joint. He was twenty-five perhaps. A bit younger than me. Both were drunk. He lived in the same house as her and as she had wine now and I had wine we drank. Poor wine and vintage wine.

She kept telling Silvano I was a famous photographer. Her head fell on my table. A forehead white and dented as old mother of pearl. I looked at Silvano, wondering what I should do and he just stared at me, eyes the points of amethyst on a seabed.

It had been a while since I slept with anyone. I tried to discourage him but I could see things by his stare, a kind of shaking loneliness, a loneliness known only to Soho, a sublimation of trees and the craft of sex and wintry mornings glaring at sex gadgets. Lily slept on one of the beds in a little side room and Silvano slept with me.

I didn't make love to him but held an Italian head of hair; his penis probing at my stomach, a colonnade of hair. In the thrust of his penis I felt, believe it or not, my mother, my father, something as simple as that, their moments before fatal injury.

Silvano came back again and again, a simple language beginning between Lily, Silvano, myself, something as commensurate as November sidling into the trees and taking articulation from them.

Lily lived now by amoral earnings, desperate Scotsmen fucking her. Her body swelled like a circus tent. She spoke of knickers, knickers gay and diverse as the colours at a Mardi Gras.

In drunkenness her obscenities lessened and she expressed the past, her past, Mayo, the island whence she came, Achill, shores by the Atlantic ocean, rocks, hills to climb, hills to look down on the sea from, hills to wonder from, to wonder if you'd escape their imprisoning terrain of church and Madonna.

'I left Dublin Bay in 1956,' she said, 'Jesus, Mary and Joseph I've never been back. But God I'd like to take a suit-case there now and camp on a beach. But sure they're probably not there any more, the beaches, the rocks, the church.

'They've probably built hotels on the shore and left the houses boarded up, the houses where they had strings of kids' bellies to feed, souls to burn, little bodies to send to England.'

They'd sent her body to England all right, sacrosanct Irish belly, nipples just over the sting of confessionals, pubic hair smelling of brine, they'd exported her to Soho.

38

Lily was one of the many Irish girls who became prostitutes in London. And Silvano, he too was a kind of prostitute. Standing outside a striptease joint, soliciting customers, his arms folded, jeans tight on his crotch, those Sicilian eyes laughing.

He'd come north from Sicily the previous winter, hitch-hiking through Naples, Rome, stopping in Paris, coming to London on a lorry, having an address or two in Earls Court, getting a job with a Cockney who owned a line of striptease joints all over England. It could have been a line of cattlemarts for thus were striptease girls treated, lambs or sheep carted about, big bottoms, lenient thighs, breasts that rose, inveigling ardour from businessmen.

He saw no contradiction in what he was doing; a young man in a paraffin-coloured jersey, eyes alight, asking only that people should come and see the show.

I was asked to photograph young women in the nude by a local retailer of the human form. I laughed, then refused. Here in Soho I was surrounded by women who dolled them-selves like chocolate boxes, to be seen, devoured like lollies.

Lily was from another time; there were women who'd do anything she said. Where she'd stop I don't know. I was never to find out. The last girlfriend I had had left me a year before and now, engaged in my work, I didn't want to be touched by women. Silvano came close, a boy, at a loss for sun, rock, snakes and the low hills, either rocky or grey, that stood before the morning light, illuminated like torches.

Come Christmas we dined together.

Lily tottered in from morning mass at Saint Patrick's in Soho. I cooked dinner. Lily had been going on and on about the Sisters of Mercy in Castlebar of late. I suspected a conversion but a conversion from what: prostitution to social security? At least she'd have her rent paid every week.

Silvano had brought an Italian friend who disappeared before I served dinner; turkey, cranberry sauce, a galaxy of vegetables.

Lily had brought wine and Silvano sherry and port.

Lily was dressed in yellow ochre; she could have been an aunt, respectable Irish like my people. She wore a black bead on her neck and after dinner she sang, like any Irish lady, a Percy French song 'The West Clare Express', standing up, her arms reaching out a little as though she was a cabaret artist.

It was a pleasant day, an unforced day.

Silvano didn't get drunk, glowed like a pool on a beach in summer. He said he was thinking of going home but a reason kept him here, flesh, fun, the gambling arcades; the hot ladies from Manchester or Liverpool. I knew I'd see him always outside a striptease joint in Soho, towards evening, a certain light in his eyes and a paraffin jersey on him catching flame.

What these two people were doing here I didn't know. We behaved like courtiers though, toasting, drinking, not getting drunk.

My past, or my heritage rather, brandished in front of me, big homes in Cork or Kerry, the Irish at sport – the Gaelic names, the songs, the wines and whiskeys. I understood a name other than my own that evening, a name born out of absolute loss, a name for experience, an enumeration of it into meaning.

After Christmas Polish women cloaked in draconian black walked poodles white as comic book snow in the gardens.

Lily I saw little of, Silvano lounged outside his striptease joint.

How long a life like this could go on I didn't know, art, work, sleep, coffees in Soho, conversations overheard: 'I live in Paris now. They appreciate me more.' 'I think I'm going to die young. I have a weak left kidney.' 'Graham commissioned me to do a play on the life of Isadora Duncan for the Gay Pride week.'

January was also a time of rugby matches and one evening Silvano tottered into my room, his nose gone purple and red and blood spouting like water from his lip. He'd been beaten up by a rugby fan from Scotland. I cleaned his face. He said he'd never go back there. I made him cocoa, looked out the window where Soho was already silent.

It was about three and we talking about Durham and Italy when a voice started up on the streets of Soho singing 'The Bells of the Angelus'. What I suspected had come to be, the slow motions towards it, a lifetime pulled away from the harshness of nuns in Mayo had reverted. Lily had gone religiously crazed, an ikon building in her of all the old saints and martyrs, the unselfishness of her mother, the prolificity of her family. The years had passed but how swiftly they were disappearing as though they hadn't counted, years of bartering your body in the gaze of Saint Patrick's in Soho. Lily was again child martyr, saint, nun's pet.

She stood by the flame in Saint Patrick's, a vigilant. She cleaned her room, inspecting every corner for dust. She got a job, cleaning floors. The paint from her hair peeled off.

We found it prematurely white.

Silvano moved in with me in February. He needed to be close to someone, anyone, his job gone, a kind of loneliness in him, just a childlike loneliness, no more than that. The radiance of spring was cutting through him too.

Lily said often that her greatest desire would have been to have had a child. Soho cleansed itself, the corners bearing advertisements for the latest films, the windows holding huge sexual gadgets.

Silvano had a job road sweeping now. He was talking about going back to Italy; the EEC had made things good for his locale, grants, and agriculture was booming. Gone was the unnerving attraction for big far off cities.

Lily had befriended a priest in Saint Patrick's and walking home one evening from visiting him she was beaten up and raped. We visited her in hospital. She didn't say much.

I could see that the shock had penetrated her and

41

absorbed something of her childhood, the pain of it, the prolificity of it, the thirteen hot water jars in the house, some leaking at irregular intervals.

She never recovered.

Perhaps she was one of the many women of the night to whom this kind of event happens, whose face is known, who abandons her profession, who walks into it unawares again.

But something gave way in her, a huge silence occurred in her and she didn't talk to me or Silvano, just stared, stared ahead, walking around Soho, walking past drunkards from Glasgow or Dublin.

Silvano took a train back to Italy one day – I loaned him some money – and the sight of Lily, her white hair blowing free, always in the garden, unnerved me; a ghost.

I left Soho but I knew her figure, her face, would always be constructed and rehabilitated within me, the lady in the gardens, gone mad a bit, silent a bit, never talking but always remembering her reasons for coming here, no money in her native land.

I was glad we'd shared some moments, that she'd sung at Christmas, that there'd been three of us to come together, however waveringly, to celebrate what it was like to know the spirit of Christmas before the curse of change came, change in movement, madness or despair.

Memories of Swinging London

Why he went there he did not know, an instinctive feel for a dull façade, an intuition borne out of time of a country unbeknownst to him now but ten years ago one of excessive rain, old stone damaged by time and trees too green, too full.

He was drunk, of course, the night he stumbled in there at ten o'clock. It had been three weeks since Marion had left him, three weeks of drink, of moronic depression, three weeks of titillating jokes with the boys at work.

Besides it had been raining that night and he'd needed shelter.

She was tired after a night's drama class when he met her, a small nun making tea with a brown kettle.

Her garb was grey and short and she spoke with a distinctive Kerry accent but yet a polish at variance with her accent.

She'd obviously been to an elocution class or two, Liam thought cynically, until he perceived her face, weary, alone, a makeshift expression of pain on it.

She'd failed that evening with her lesson she said. Nothing had happened, a half dozen boys from Roscommon and Leitrim had left the hall uninspired.

Then she looked at Liam as though wondering who she was speaking to anyway, an Irish drunk, albeit a well dressed one. In fact he was particularly well dressed that evening, wearing a neatly cut grey suit and a white shirt, spotless but for some dots of Guinness.

They talked with some reassurance when he was less drunk. He sat back as she poured tea.

She was from Kerry she said, West Kerry. She'd been a few months in Africa and a few months in the United States but this was her first real assignment, other than a while as domestic science teacher in a Kerry convent. Here she was all of nurse, domestic and teacher. She taught young men from Mayo and Roscommon how to move; she had become keen on drama while going to college in Dublin. She'd pursued this interest while teaching domestic science in Kerry, an occupation she was ill qualified for, having studied English literature in Dublin.

'I'm a kind of social worker,' she said, 'I'm given these lads to work with. They come here looking for something. I give them drama.'

She'd directed Eugene O'Neill in West Kerry, she'd directed Arthur Miller in West Kerry. She'd moulded young men there but a different kind of young men, bank clerks. Here she was landed with labourers, drunks.

'How did you come by this job?' Liam asked.

She looked at him, puzzled by his directness.

'They were looking for a suitable spot to put an ardent Sister of Mercy,' she said.

There was a lemon iced cake in a corner of the room and she caught his eye spying it and she asked him if he'd like some, apologizing for not offering him some earlier. She made quite a ceremony of cutting it, dishing it up on a blue rimmed plate.

He picked at it.

'And you,' she said, 'What part of Ireland do you come from?'

He had to think about it for a moment. It had been so long. How could he tell her about limestone streets and dank trees? How could he convince her he wasn't lying when he spun yarns about an adolescence long gone?

'I come from Galway,' he said, 'from Ballinasloe.'

44

'My father used to go to the horse fair there,' she said. And then she was off again about Kerry and farms, until suddenly she realized it should be him that should be speaking.

She looked at him but he said nothing.

He was peaceful. He had a cup of tea, a little bit of lemon cake left.

'How long have you been here?' she asked.

'Ten years.'

He was unforthcoming with answers.

The aftermath of drink had left his body and he was sitting as he had not sat for weeks, consuming tea, peaceful. In fact, when he thought of it, he hadn't been like this for years, sitting quietly, untortured by memories of Ireland but easy with them, memories of green and limestone grey.

She invited him back and he didn't come back for days. But as always in the case of two people who meet and genuinely like one another they were destined to meet again.

He saw her in Camden town one evening, knew that his proclivity to Keats and Byron at school was somehow justified. She was unrushed, carrying vegetables, asked him why he had not come. He told her he'd been intending to come, that he was going to come. She smiled. She had to go she said. She was firm.

Afterwards he drank, one pint of Guinness. He would go back he told himself.

In fact it was as though he was led by some force of persuasion, easiness of language which existed between him and Sister Sarah, a lack of embarrassment at silence.

He took a bus from his part of Shepherd's Bush to Camden Town. Rain slashed, knifing the evening with black. The first instinct he had was to get a return bus but unnerved he went on.

Entering the centre the atmosphere was suddenly appropriated by music, Tchaikovsky, *Swan Lake*. He entered the

45

hall to see a half dozen young men in black jerseys, blue trousers, dying, quite genuinely like swans.

She saw him. He saw her. She didn't stop the procedure, merely acknowledged him and went on, her voice reverberating in the hall, to talk of movement, of the necessity to identify the real lines in one's body and flow with them.

Yes, he'd always recall that, 'The real lines in one's body.' When she had stopped talking she approached him. He stood there, aware that he was a stranger, not in a black jersey.

Then she wound up the night's procedure with more music, this time Beethoven, and the young men from Roscommon and Mayo behaved like constrained ballerinas as they simulated dusk.

Afterwards they spoke again. In the little kitchen.

'Dusk is a word for balance between night and day,' she said. 'I asked them to be relaxed, to be aware of time flowing through them.'

The little nun had an errand to make.

Alone, there, Liam smoked a cigarette. He thought of Marion, his wife gone north to Leeds, fatigued with him, with marriage, with the odd affair. She had worked as a receptionist in a theatre.

She'd given up her job, gone home to Mummy, left the big city for the northern smoke. In short her marriage had ended.

Looking at the litter-bin Liam realized how much closer to accepting this fact he'd come. Somehow he'd once thought marriage to be for life but here it was, one marriage dissolved and nights to fill, a body to shelter, a life to lead.

A young man with curly blond hair entered. He was looking for Sister Sarah. He stopped when he saw Liam, taken aback. These boys were like a special battalion of guards in their black jerseys. He was an intruder, cool, English almost, his face, his features relaxed, not rough or ruddy. The young man said he was from Roscommon. That was near Liam's home.

He spoke of farms, of pigs, said he'd had to leave, come to the city, search for neon. Now he'd found it. He'd never go back to the country. He was happy here, big city, many people, a dirty river and a population of people which included all races.

'I miss the dances though,' the boy said, 'the dances of Sunday nights. There's nothing like them in London, the cars all pulled up and the ballroom jiving with music by Big Tom and the Mainliners. You miss them in London but there are other things that compensate.'

When asked by Liam what compensated most for the loss of fresh Sunday night dancehalls amid green fields the boy said, 'The freedom.'

Sister Sarah entered, smiled at the boy, sat down with Liam. The boy questioned her about a play they were intending to do and left, turning around to smile at Liam.

Sarah – her name came to him without the prefix now – spoke about the necessity of drama in schools, in education.

'It is a liberating force,' she said. 'It brings out—' she paused '—the swallow in people.'

And they both laughed, amused and gratified at the absurdity of the description.

Afterwards he perceived her in a hallway alone, a nun in a short outfit, considering the after-effects of her words that evening, pausing before plunging the place into darkness.

He told her he would return and this time he did, sitting among boys from Roscommon and Tipperary, improvising situations. She called on him to be a soldier returning from war and this he did, embarrassedly, recalling that he too was a soldier once, a boy outside a barracks in Ireland, beside a bed of crocuses. People smiled at his shattered innocence, at this attempt at improvisation. Sister Sarah reserved a smile. In the middle of a simulated march he stopped.

'I can't. I can't,' he said.

People smiled, let him be.

He walked to the bus-stop, alone. Rain was edging him in, winter was coming. It hurt with its severity tonight. He passed a sex-shop, neon light dancing over the instruments in the window. The pornographic smile of a British comedian looked out from a newsagent's.

He got his bus.

Sleep took him in Shepherd's Bush. He dreamt of a school long ago in County Galway which he attended for a few years, urns standing about the remains of a Georgian past.

At work people noticed he was changing. They noticed a greater serenity. An easiness about the way he was holding a cup. They virtually chastised him for it.

Martha McPherson looked at him, said sarcastically, 'You look hopeful.'

He was thinking of Keats in the canteen when she spoke to him, of words long ago, phrases from mouldering books at school at the beginning of autumn.

His flat was tidier now; there was a space for books which had not hitherto been there. He began a letter home, stopped, couldn't envisage his mother, old woman by a sea of bog.

Sister Sarah announced plans for a play they would perform at Christmas. The play would be improvised, bit by bit, and she asked for suggestions about the content.

One boy from Leitrim said, 'Let's have a play about the tinkers.'

Liam was cast for a part as tinker king and bit by bit over the weeks he tried, tried to push off shyness, act out little scenes.

People laughed at him. He felt humiliated, twisted inside. Yet he went on.

His face was moulding, clearer than before, and in his eyes was a piercing darkness. He made speeches, trying to

48

recall the way the tinkers spoke at home, long lines of them on winter evenings, camps in country lanes, smoke rising as a sun set over distant steeples.

He spoke less to colleagues, more to himself, phrasing and rephrasing old questions, wondering why he had left Ireland in the first place, a boy, sixteen, lonely, very lonely on a boat making its way through a winter night.

'I suppose I left Ireland,' he told Sister Sarah one night, 'because I felt ineffectual, totally ineffectual. The priests at school despised my independence. My mother worked as a char. My father was dead. I was a mature youngster who liked women, had one friend at school, a boy who wrote poetry.

'I came to England seeking reasons for living. I stayed with my older brother who worked in a factory.

'My first week in England a Greek homosexual who lived upstairs asked me to sleep with him. That ended my innocence. I grew up somewhere around then, became adult very, very young.'

1966, the year he left Ireland.

Sonny and Cher sang 'I've got you, babe.'

London was readying itself for blossoming, the Swinging Sixties had attuned themselves to Carnaby Street, to discothèques, to parks. Ties looked like huge flowers, young hippies sat in parks. And in 1967, the year 'Sergeant Pepper's Lonely Hearts' Band' appeared, a generation of young men with horned-rimmed glasses looking like John Lennon. 'It was like a party,' Liam said, 'a continual party. I ate, drank at this feast.

'Then I met Marion. We married in 1969, the year Brian Jones died. I suppose we spent our honeymoon at his funeral. Or at least in Hyde Park where Mick Jagger read a poem in commemoration of him. "Weep no more for Adonais is not dead." '

Sister Sarah smiled. She obviously liked romantic poetry too, she didn't say anything, just looked at him, with a long

49

slow smile. 'I understand,' she said, though what she was referring to he didn't know.

Images came clearer now, Ireland, the forty steps at school, remnants of a Georgian past, early mistresses, most of all the poems of Keats and Shelley.

Apart from the priests, there had been things about school he'd enjoyed, the images in poems, the celebration of love and laughter by Keats and Shelley, the excitement at finding a new poem in a book.

She didn't say much to him these days, just looked at him. He was beginning to fall into place, to be whole in this environment of rough and ready young men.

Somehow she had seduced him.

He wore clean cool casual white shirts now, looked faraway at work, hair drifting over his forehead as in adolescence. Someone noticed his clear blue eyes and remarked on them, Irish eyes, and he knew this identification as Irish had not been so absolute for years.

' "They came like swallows and like swallows went," ' Sister Sarah quoted one evening. It was a fragment from a poem by Yeats, referring to Coole Park, a place not far from Liam's home, where the legendary Irish writers convened, Yeats, Synge, Lady Gregory, O'Casey, a host of others, leaving their mark in a place of growth, of bark, of spindly virgin trees. And in a way now Liam associated himself with this horde of shadowy and evasive figures; he was Irish. For that reason alone he had strength now. He came from a country vilified in England but one which, generation after generation, had produced genius, and observation of an extraordinary kind.

Sister Sarah made people do extraordinary things, dance, sing, boys dress as girls, grown men jump over one another like children. She had Liam festoon himself in old clothes, with paper flowers in his hat.

The story of the play ran like this:

Two tinker families are warring. A boy from one falls in

50

love with a girl from the other. They run away and are pursued by Liam who plays King of the Tinkers. He eventually finds them but they kill themselves rather than part and are buried with the King of the Tinkers making a speech about man's greed and folly.

No one questioned that it was too mournful a play for Christmas; there were many funny scenes, wakes, fights, horse-stealing and the final speech, words of which flowed from Liam's mouth, had a beauty, an elegance which made young men from Roscommon who were accustomed to hefty Irish showband singers stop and be amazed at the beauty of language.

Towards the night the play was to run Sister Sarah became a little irritated, a little tired. She'd been working too hard, teaching during the day. She didn't talk to Liam much and he felt hurt and disorganized. He didn't turn up for rehearsal for two nights running. He rang and said he was ill.

He threw a party. All his former friends arrived and Marion's friends. The flat churned with people. Records smashed against the night. People danced. Liam wore an open neck collar-less white shirt. A silver cross was dangling, one picked up from a craft shop in Cornwall.

In the course of the party a girl became very, very drunk and began weeping about an abortion she'd had. She sat in the middle of the floor, crying uproariously, awaiting the arrival of someone.

Eventually Liam moved towards her, took her in his arms, offered her a cup of tea. She quietened. 'Thank you,' she said simply.

The crowds went home. Bottles were left everywhere. Liam took his coat, walked to an all-night café and, as he didn't have to work, watched the dawn come.

She didn't chastise him. Things went on as normal. He played his part, dressed in ridiculous clothes. Sister Sarah was in a lighter mood. She drank a sherry with Liam one evening, one cold December evening. As it was coming near Christmas she spoke of festivity in Kerry. Cross-road dances in Dun Caoin, the mirth of Kerry which had never died. She told Liam how her father would take her by car to church on Easter Saturday, how they'd watch the waters being blessed and later dance at the cross-roads, melodions playing and the Irish fiddle.

There had been nothing like that in Liam's youth. He'd come from the Midlands, dull green, statues of Mary outside factories. He'd been privileged to know defeat from an early age.

'You should go to Kerry some time,' Sister Sarah said.

'I'd like to,' Liam said, 'I'd like to. But it's too late now.'

Yet when the musicians came to rehearse the music Liam knew it was not too late. He may have missed the West of Ireland in his youth, the simplicity of a Gaelic people but here now in London, melodions exploding, he was in an Ireland he'd never known, the extreme West, gullies, caves, peninsulas, roads winding into desecrated hills and clouds always coming in. 'Imagine,' he thought, 'I've never even seen the sea.'

He told her one night about the fiftieth anniversary of the 1916 revolution which had occurred before he left, old priests at school fumbling with words about dead heroes, bedraggled tricolours flying over the school and young priests, beautiful in the extreme, reciting the poetry of Patrick Pearse.

'When the bombs came in England,' Liam said, 'and we were blamed, the ordinary Irish working people, I knew they were to blame, those priests, the people who lied about glorious deeds. Violence is never, ever glorious.'

He met her in a café for coffee one day and she laughed and said it was almost like having an affair. She said she'd once fancied a boy in Kerry, a boy she was directing in *All My Sons*. He had bushy blond hair, kept Renoir reproductions on his wall, was a bank clerk. 'But he went off with another girl,' she said, 'and broke my heart.'

He met her in Soho Square Gardens one day and they walked together. She spoke of Africa and the States, travelling, the mission of the modern church, the redemption of souls lost in a mire of nonchalance. On Tottenham Court Road she said goodbye to him.

'See you next rehearsal,' she said.

He stood there when she left and wanted to tell her she'd awakened in him a desire for a country long forgotten, an awareness of another side of that country, music, drama, levity but there was no saying these things.

When the night of the play finally arrived he acted his part well. But all the time, all the time he kept an eye out for her.

Afterwards there were celebrations, balloons dancing, Irish bankers getting drunk. He sat and waited for her to come to him and when she didn't rose and looked for her.

She was speaking to an elderly Irish labourer.

He stood there, patiently, for a moment. He wanted her to tell him about Christmas lights in Ireland long ago, about the music of O'Riada and the southern going whales. But she persevered in speaking to this old man about Christmas in Kerry.

Eventually he danced with her. She held his arm softly. He knew now he was in love with her and didn't know how to put it to her. She left him and talked to some other people.

Later she danced again with him. It was as though she saw something in his eyes, something forbidding.

'I have to go now,' she said as the music still played. She touched his arm gently, moved away. His eyes searched for her afterwards but couldn't find her. Young men he'd acted with came up and started clapping him on the back. They joked and they laughed. Suddenly Liam found he was getting sick. He didn't make for the lavatory. He went instead to the street. There he vomited. It was raining. He got very wet going home.

At Christmas he went to midnight mass in Westminster Cathedral, a thing he had never done before. He stood with women in mink coats and Irish char-women as the choir sang 'Come all ye faithful'. He had Christmas with an old aunt and at midday rang Marion. They didn't say much to one another that day but after Christmas she came to see him.

One evening they slept together. They made love as they had not for years, he entering her deeply, resonantly, thinking of Galway long ago, a river where they swam as children.

She stayed after Christmas. They were more subdued with one another. Marion was pregnant. She worked for a while and when her pregnancy became too obvious she ceased working.

She walked a lot. He wondered at a woman, his wife, how he hadn't noticed before how beautiful she looked. They were passing Camden Town one day when he recalled a nun he'd once known. He told Marion about her, asked her to enter with him, went in a door, asked for Sister Sarah.

Someone he didn't recognise told him she'd gone to Nigeria, that she'd chosen the African sun to boys in black jerseys. He wanted to follow her for one blind moment, to tell her that people like her were too rare to be lost but knew no words of his would convince her. He took his wife's hand and went about his life, quieter than he had been before.

Cats

He came in the summer, left Dublin, city of hippies, of Divine Light people, flowers before an altar in Santry, oranges before the same altar and rhubarb. He'd lived with the Divine Light for a while and now, disillusioned, left, seeking fresh pastures. Dermot Cleary arrived in London early in the summer of 1972, a boy from Dublin, unsure. He stayed with Divine Light people in Richmond, using them though distrusting them and one evening walking by the Thames he encountered Delia. She was watching a troop of swans and it was that which brought them together, a troop of swans which distilled a sense of absolute stillness in both of them. They met through stillness.

She remarked, 'Swans are aristocratic birds. They suit Richmond.' She had an English accent but when she discovered he was Irish she told him she was Irish too, from Belfast.

He went to see her one day he wasn't working in a pet shop. She lived in an elegant flat in Richmond. It was the cats which ensnared him first, a myriad of them crawling like mice. She introduced five, forewent saying anything about any others.

He sat and had tea with her, the water of the Thames creating exultant and swaying motions on the walls.

She was from Belfast, she repeated, where tea was strong. When asked what she did she replied that her family had left her rich. Dermot looked about and noticed photographs, old photographs like bullion gold of girls in forties dresses with raised sleeves in indistinguishable parts of Ireland. Delia told him she'd been a poet, used to read her poetry on the BBC. On closer inspection the walls held photographs of forties English poets signed by themselves. Delia had had quite a reputation in her day, less as a poet, more as a friend to many poets. Now she'd abandoned friendship like an old armchair and sat, an exile, a conscious portrait.

Dermot had grown up in the poorest part of Dublin, joined a skinhead gang at nine, at thirteen was studying Euripides and Aristophanes in the National Library, having finished at school at twelve. He worked in the docks, joined a union like his father; at nineteen, disturbed by mystical mischief, he joined the Divine Light and so left his job, haunted Dublin's middle-class venues, the Coffee Inn, Bewley's, mixing with students and civil servants over coffee and chips and wine. Someone said one night in the Coffee Inn under a collage of photographs of Rome, 'We're living in a lasting city.' And it was for a while, city of canals and waterfalls where you dived on summer days, city of reefers and a plethora of gurus, all grabbing the soul of the city's young and diverting them from the poverty and the waste to astral visions and the whine of a saxophone at the top of Grafton Street.

Dermot wondered what made him leave: a certain fatigue with daily pleasures, a restlessness with a culture of dope and smiles and inter-relationships that tried its best to forget.

A young negro singer lay on the Green the day he left. A country girl challenged Grafton Street in jeans. Some Divine Light people basked over iced coffee in tall slim glasses in Bewley's. Dublin was dictated by a spell; a whore motivated by a rich man. Dermot took the mail boat from the place where he used to work. Arriving in London was arriving in another city and at that stage he began to realize there were no lasting cities, for in London too it was summer, and in London too there was the same yearning among the people he stayed with.

Delia reclined in her chair one day. She spoke very slowly about her youth in Belfast, emphasising every word. She'd grown up outside Belfast, her father a rich man and a widower. He'd owned a factory and raised her, a daughter he sent to a free school. He was a Quaker and believed in all kinds of enterprises, taking her every Easter to Nice. He was mother and father to her, an effeminate man wrapped in fair isle jerseys. When she was seventeen he'd seduced her. She'd left for Paris, studied painting. Then after her father's death, he dying in a welter of guilt, she came back to England, befriended poet and painter. Now she just lived, lived on an inheritance.

Of course there were her cats, crawling about the place, each with a name, an invocation, eyes emerald or opal, looking at Dermot quizzically. When she questioned herself, she said, about life's greatest loss, it was the loss of love, though in her case it was different because her lover had been her father, a man who dabbled in plants and with young boys. Delia sat back like a poet purging herself of her past; her eyes closed and an inner focus on some torment. Lovers, cats maybe, beings who had caused her pain.

She was like a door opening to another world for him, a milestone at Damascus for him, the woman now who led her cats like a medieval procession by the Thames. He didn't really believe the tale about her father but he didn't really disbelieve it either. It was obvious she'd experienced disengagement in her youth, from her father, Ireland, sanity; she came from a different Ireland from his, one that he'd hardly realized had existed, but given it, he accepted it, her world of Irish painters, poets and Quakers. And with these elements were her Protestantism, her Unionism, her acknowledgement even if not directly of a world of suppression. She'd hardly touched on the South of Ireland, had just known some poets and painters and a fat nun who conducted choirs. Delia McCaughey behaved like someone who'd contributed a lifetime to art and was now relaxing, albeit with memories that stung her eyes and her cheekbones and her lips, sometimes curled from a kind of agony.

If the Divine Light people attained to God they certainly showed nothing of God to him, becoming jealous of his relationship with Delia and suspicious of it, ostracising him in small ways, denying him cornflakes in the morning.

In July Dermot Cleary moved in with Delia McCaughey. He worked in his pet shop. She made endless cups of tea. They walked in the long evenings, followed by cats. She drank, became tipsy, whined and one Saturday afternoon by the Thames watching a child, whose mother called him Merlin, Delia quoted a friend of hers 'And death shall have no dominion'. They planned to go off to Nice together in the autumn. He had his little bed. She had her big bed in another room.

The tortoises coughed at work, parrots demanded, budgies battered his ears. The world turned into a menagerie for Dermot that summer, hippies, aristocrats, cats. More than anything Delia's cats like the diffuse part of herself. Despite her endless literacy and artistic friends of the past, despite all the drink poured on them and the banquets provided for them none came to see her now and perhaps there was a more serious wound than her father's seduction of her. All she had was her cats.

But now she had Dermot, ex-skinhead, in blue jeans, with coal black hair and eyes even deeper, blacker jade.

Dermot had a black haired and a black eyed family, their hair and eyes profoundly black, their natures profoundly generous despite their cooped up state in a tiny council flat. The whole family had showered importance on him, his education, but he'd rejected them and gone to the flats of Rathmines and Rathgar. Maybe, Delia, this odd Protestant, was his way back.

If she'd been a bit younger he would have seduced her but there was something forbidding about her flesh, early in the morning ashen, a thousand cigarettes stubbed in her. He'd

58

had a few girlfriends, a close relationship with a boy but this was the first time he'd lived with someone like this, morning, noon and night. It never occurred to either of them it was strange; she spoke about his favourite preoccupation, poetry, Ezra Pound, Dylan Thomas, Louis MacNeice.

He wrote verses that summer which she read in a loud elegant voice as though speaking to ghosts three decades before and trying to redress something. The cats strangled their miaows for these moments, acknowledging the intensity. He wore red check shirts and his hair grew longer, 'Byronesque,' she said. It was a nice summer. He didn't know where he was going but it didn't matter, there were poems to write while venerable poets of the forties looked down on him. One he wrote about a lasting city; it wasn't Dublin or London but a city beyond, a city of the imagination where time stopped still, Richmond on a summer's evening, the Grand Canal, Dublin, on a summer's afternoon, the waterfall splashing with light and children rolling into it like berries. All the time he was conscious of the photographs of poets, autographs and dates on their tweed ties. This time was signed too, by a mutual autograph, his and Delia's.

She rarely spoke about the Northern troubles but when she did it was as if they were happening to a country other than the one she'd known. Her father and herself had created magic from capitalism, these bombs, these deaths, they were a nuisance. If she was flippant she was also most definitely Protestant, nonconformist, a little bit bigoted, neat in her endeavours. Her flat, though she was frail, was immaculate and her father had been hardworking, thus driving her on to her own life once, scribbling verse. Her typewriter stood like a museum piece now. Her Oxford dictionary was seated. No poems were left. A few eccentric magazines. That was all.

And of her father's home it was constantly being battered. She didn't remember bigotry but she suggested it in small ways, her elitism, her fondness for good-looking people. His hair grew longer, no longer skinhead or guru follower. He wore a cravat. She took him to dinner, she wearing black gloves sequined here and there with gold, ordering Italian wine. He was her audience. He was recording her words.

She told him about other love affairs she'd had but always returned to the point where she discussed her father and how gradually it became obvious to her that she could not go home, that it was true, that they knew, the others of her family. Her father and she in the late thirties in Nice, a love affair, a divination of romance against a warped and endlessly cruel environment. Delia and her father had made love, not once but more than once, many times. She'd gone to the poets and the artists, leaving her father with a fetish for farmboys. Delia McCaughey had created her own crucifix against Irish history. He'd died, he'd been buried, after the war, and they'd shunned her, the others. Then eventually too as she withered and grew older the poets left her. She'd been a flower of fashion.

Dermot wrote many poems that summer, poems as though compelled to speed. Something was closing in on him. They came. Delia criticised them. The cats watched.

Eventually he gave up work and she supported him. He tidied. She made meals. Then one day he returned and found her dead.

It all seemed so strange, years later, a kind of grotesque. Dermot returned to Ireland, abandoning his poetry and his guru, becoming involved in politics. Perhaps that's why he'd written poetry with such speed that summer. Social problems grabbed him. The waste of central Dublin. But he knew he had created his crucifix too. He worked with the poor, the destitute, lyrics no longer came to him. But somehow her lyricism resounded, something turning a harsh political meeting to gold.

It was like a question posed that summer, an unnameable gesture made. Somehow the Marxist terminology couldn't

60

solidify too hard because she haunted him, her moment of death, the dignity of her face in death, the attitude that death, try as hard as it could, couldn't have dominion because they'd made a mutual speech, because they tried even for a short time to decipher words unfinished from a past which blurred into signed photographs and posed faces.

Children of Lir

The young man came back to Ireland at Christmas. He'd
spent the previous few months in Rome. His eyes had
hollowed a little, they looked grimmer, more searching.
He'd lived in a flat off Campo dei Fiori with an American
boy, cries of fruit vendors outside, torpor of wet marigolds.
Rome had exploded towards winter, wine in the evenings,
amethyst skies, skies smouldering with memories of cruel
emperors. Under the statue of Bruno, truant monk, young
hippies waited regardless of history. They were a sacramental lot, full of silence and expectancy. Music and drugs were
religion to them; there was no sex, a banishment of desire.
Desmond had slept beside an American boy from California
platonically; he'd had some money from his summer
working in London. Jesse was from Pacifica, rich boy; he
dug heroin into the pale part of his Californian arm.
Desmond had wanted to help him but Jesse's inability was
chosen, an intense self-protective zone. His eyes would rise
with an appeal but the appeal was deadened by a kind of
despair. 'In California,' Jesse said, 'you are given despair.
Sun, a surf-board, despair.' When asked by a boy from
County Galway what he meant Jesse spoke of a mother who
grabbed his friends into her flesh; a father who'd seduced
him when he was thirteen. His sister was in religion, his
mother now in love with a film director, his father making
sex films and he swooning here to heroin. Desmond looked
back on his own adolescence and remembered the frozen
evenings, the odd trips to Dublin from Ballinasloe, the neon

lights smashing the night, smashing the peculiar snow storms of Dublin, smashing an endless skyline and an endless loneliness. He told Jesse he'd always been haunted by city lights since then. Rome was the ultimate city, lights on a fountain at night, the Coliseum lighted up, lights from a trattoria reflected in a young hippy's eyes. Music stirred up, an occasional ripple, Deep Purple, Rossini. The young man from Galway veered towards heroin but that drug was not necessary; there were other tremulous opiates, memory, a desire to kill the past.

You walked in the Borghese gardens at nights and time stood still; for moments, hours he fled time and identity. But it came as no surprise that there was always a return to self.

He'd come to Italy seeking the beach where Shelley's body had been washed up, found the place where Byron swam instead. Rome too fondled Keats' House and the grave of Keats in the Protestant cemetery. Autumn had veered into winter, a haze over the Tiber, a burning throbbing light like a compelling vision. The vision led to this, a boat to Ireland, his girlfriend's arms. She'd changed; she'd been having an affair. 'Tell me about Rome,' she said. He said nothing at first, then smiled. 'It really is the eternal city,' he said.

January was bleak in Dublin, full of haggard hippies, their Afghan coats torn. The Liffey was high, slivers of snow always in the air, prodding fingers of hail. The Liffey was mesmerised by its own gloom, the skies were low. You hugged yourself by a fire. Always conscious that a boat led out of here again.

Until now Dublin had been drugs and the trees of Stephen's Green in summer, the radiant postures of young men from housing estates, the music of demanding guitars. Now he was faced with getting a job. His girlfriend stayed away from him, a mask in the January cold, a harlequin. He looked through the papers. He'd never used his degree from University College but now he rang up schools. A very

63

draconian voice in a school in the Liberties was positive about prospects. Desmond went for an interview. The building was red like a public lavatory. Yes, he'd have no difficulty in being given a job. He looked the part; a mellifluous Italian autumn still within him, the surgence of English romantic poetry. In a tweed jacket Desmond was told he'd be employed. He looked to the January sky and perceived a snowflake flickering. It didn't look too promising but then the Dublin sky was a contagion of moods. Today outside a vocational school it was grey and frozen and solidified, a barrier. The barrier against the past, against happiness, against the outside world.

His former friends still walked along the Liffey in tattered Afghan coats. A few were arrested on drugs charges. The more cautious stayed at home and smoked marijuana in their bedrooms. Desmond's relationship with the outside world was not the best either but he journeyed from Belgrave Square with its sombre passing buses to school each morning. He had a routine.

The school was awful. It embodied not just the worst in Irish society but every imaginary evil in a Marxist diction-ary. Young Dublin working-class children captive to foolish, ignorant, half-educated country teachers. No knowledge was imparted. A kind of sadism enacted. It was as if these children were cubs in the Dublin zoo. Only one teacher stood out, a monk, full of grace and a radiant gentleness. He walked the red corridors with kindness. The children respected him. He was an aimiable, laughing man from Whitefriar Street church, monks who traditionally associat-ed themselves with the Dublin poor. His solitary triumph was difficult to explain; his eyes were brown like his garb and compassionate. Compassion was a difficult state and as such the children veered towards him as to a source.

The first day in the school Desmond had his children improvise a café scene, but, as so often happened in their cafés, violence exploded. Next moment they were on top of

64

one another on the floor when the headmaster walked in. It was with difficulty Desmond explained it was a drama lesson.

The headmaster had him teach English from mouldering, death-soaked grammar books. That was fine for a time while the headmaster looked in. Then he took Frank O'Connor's early stories to school and read them. The boys loved them. Outside gulls performed somersaults. His children, especially the younger ones, were wild and unruly. A prostitute would sometimes come to the yard outside and call up, a mad local girl who seduced fifteen-year-olds. The class would explode. The headmaster couldn't get rid of her. She was as frequent as Saint Bernadette's sight of Our Lady. She was hard done for customers these days.

Another day John Miflin came to school with an alsatian. The alsatian galloped down the corridor and attacked the secretary, pulling off a little bit of her green felt skirt. John was taken to a concentration camp in the North, a borstal near the Northern border.

It was a lonely occupation, teaching, especially when you disavowed the system. He wouldn't stay here long, time to make a little money, to form some ideas on Ireland, to view the system outside the safety of university. Something was going from Desmond's life, order, like a child letting go of his hand. These, despite the disorderliness of the children, were the last weeks of profound order in his life. His girlfriend's brow was arched. She had plans of leaving.

Still there were comforts, Bewley's restaurant which wasn't too far, the *Irish Times* in the morning, walnut cakes. He didn't talk to the survivors of Morocco and Katmandu. He deigned to be alone.

Stephane Grapelli came to town and so did Van Morrison. Van Morrison looked ill. He stuttered over his songs. It was as though a cough was in control of him. Desmond's image of consumptive English poets returned. It was as if this whole city was seized by consumption and the last

65

shreds of romanticism were dying. Young people walked by the Liffey, bent on going away again, to the south, to the sun. In short Dublin's hippy euphoria was over.

He'd never been a hippy but he'd been introduced to their world by his girlfriend. He'd smoked dope with them and listened to their music. But Dublin had meant more to him, an order of the soul, the gatherings of religious groups, the Grand Canal on a summer's day, urchins diving into it and the regal Georgian houses suffused in amber. He was essentially a country boy who'd come to the city. At first he'd been lonely here but then he'd met young people, mad young people full of games and notions of discovery. Now they were emptying into other places. A cold wind blew, the Irish flag shuffled a bit; the music of Stephane Grapelli reached a staccato over a city of manoeuvring buses and people returning from work. The vision was nearly gone from their gait.

Teaching in an all boys' vocational school in a poorer part of Dublin gave Desmond many ideas about this society, how the poor were twisted and wrung and how politics were dominated by seedy people from the country. These children were deprived of any dreams. They weren't middle class so therefore weren't told about Keats or Parnell. They were given the basics and if they didn't learn they were batoned.

Desmond wore more adventurous clothes now, scarlet shirts, black jackets; the boys called him 'Ducky', maybe because of his eyes, his clothes, his voice a bit shattered. He didn't care. Come March he spoke to a little boy who said he had found Brendan Behan's body and, as it was the tenth anniversary of Brendan Behan's death and seeing that Behan was from here, they had an anniversary ceremony, flowers on the table and a reading from Brendan Behan's poems and plays. The boys began slowly to respect him; they loved the sacramental. Holy Communions, confirmations, weddings. Now they saw they could forge sacrament from life. They prayed for Brendan Behan, fallen Irishman.

66

The sun came. The year eased. Had it been a last flake of snow that flew past a window or just a gull when Desmond read from Brendan Behan? The colours of Dublin resumed. Hands fondled hands, struggling to renew warmth in those hands. Stephen's Green flourished, a lightness came, a suspension.

After Easter Desmond returned to school. Now a funny thing had been happening. The boys had been continually telling him that a boy in another class had told them that Desmond had confessed his love for him. Desmond didn't know what they were talking about but before Easter he'd begun to notice a boy, about fifteen, in the corridor always eyeing him, a boy with sturdy chestnut hair, usually in a tomato coloured jersey. His presence in the corridor suggested a catalogue of misdemeanours. He had an inquisitive eye which often flashed with humour even as he looked at Desmond. But it wasn't until after Easter that this boy began following Desmond up the street to Bewley's in the afternoons, straggling along by the wall. He would never come into Bewley's, just watch from a distance. Sometimes Desmond would stop and look behind. The boy too would stop and look like a lame girl Desmond knew as a child in Ballinasloe who was obsessed with him. May had come to the Green. Desmond recited Shakespeare to his girlfriend one day, 'Shall I compare thee to a summer's day?' only to find three of his class behind the bush. She was dangling with him again, uncertain. Together they dressed to the hilt and took to the pubs at night. Despite the superficiality of these pubs Dublin blossomed as he had never seen it before, the summer streets, the crowds loitering outside the pubs, the gaiety, the abandon that had become a reverberation of a last strategy of forgetfulness. His girlfriend wandered in and out of his life and one day, while she was off with another boy, the child from school approached him in Bewley's. He sat down beside him, having followed him from school. At first he didn't say anything, then he told Desmond his name

67

was Miles. Desmond bought him coffee. They sliced a walnut cake in half and ate it. Miles looked around suspiciously. 'I'm an orphan,' he said. 'Who do you live with?' Desmond asked. 'My mother.' 'Then you're not an orphan.' 'My father's dead.' 'I see.' There was silence. Miles said, 'Mammy says you can come and have tea with us some day.' 'I'd like to.' 'I must go now.' The boy made off with a satchel.

Now it was Desmond's turn to follow the boy with the mask-like face, the hair shaped like a medieval monk's and edged with almond, the serious eyes and altogether the sense he could be snatched from one of the medieval tombs of the Liberties, an embalmed body. Now it was Desmond's turn to be inquisitive. He no longer saw Miles on the corridor and it was he who had to do the seeking. Around them he could hear pigs squealing. Nearby was a tannery. Miles did a little disappearing act and all Desmond could do was look out the window at Saint Patrick's cathedral, a spiral. He read Saint John of the Cross under a Chagall reproduction in his bedsit. He planned for the summer, a trip abroad. He wore nice orderly jerseys. Then Miles reappeared and confirmed the invitation to tea, the address, the time.

His mother waited in a council flat. A dumpy woman, hair tinged like marmalade. Miles sat beside her, wearing a white, newly laundered shirt. The first thing she declared was gratitude for the special interest Desmond took in Miles, not realizing Desmond had never even taught him. Miles was silent. She told Desmond over bacon and cabbage that she was an unmarried mother, had begot Miles in Liverpool where she'd worked as a prostitute. She'd come back to Ireland but no one was friendly to her. It was great to hear of someone being kind to her son. She'd come back because she missed home, the Liberties, the decrepit, encased statues of Mary, the buildings smelling like latrines, the grave of Dean Swift nearby and those of

68

other luminaries, this odd mixture of annihilation and sublime beauty.

Miles sat impassively. 'Miles told me his father was dead,' Desmond said. 'Oh yes, I lived with him for a while in Liverpool. Then he went off. Got a boat. He died in Singapore. Got some tropical disease. We were never married, a lad from the Coombe. What you country people don't realize is that us Dubliners, real Dubliners, are wanderers too.'

'I'm worried,' the woman said coming closer, 'worried about Miles. It's lonely. He doesn't have friends. When Miles told me about you I thought, "Well here's a chance." You see he's interested in going places, seeing museums, but there's no one to take him.' Desmond knew what she was suggesting; he also knew that this fattish lady still practised her trade. 'Where does Miles want to go specifically?' 'Well, I think more than anything he'd like to see the Rock of Cashel.'

Desmond didn't know if they were both crazy; he accepted them. The boy had books about Celtic kings and the archaeological wonders of Ireland. He wondered what he should do. His girlfriend was engrossed in her affair. Miles sat there like a triumphant aristocrat, lips barely moving and pouted.

'You see,' his mother said, 'no one in this country cares.' Desmond realized he'd gone back to school to learn; now he'd been taught this supreme lesson. Ireland was not a place where you could surmount ultimate obstacles, you could go so far. A boy, his mother here, both apparently mad, were merely an indication that people smiled more in Rome. He wanted to tell his girlfriend about it; she was a student of Fritz Perls but she was engrossed in other things. Then Desmond had the idea of leading the whole school like the children's crusade to the Rock of Cashel. Miles wasn't really a child. In fact he was shaping into young adulthood with alarming interest. Desmond intuited Grapelli's

69

violin again, a clear divination. This was life, the tremulous heart of a hidden Ireland, mother a prostitute, boy a little handsome antiquarian.

Desmond went to see them often. Miles' mother spoke of Liverpool, her days there, rearing Miles, always her eye on the Irish sea. She made him Dublin coddle and sang 'Molly Malone' for him. Miles read peacefully; Desmond's presence was a reassurance. Desmond told Miles' mother about his girlfriend off after other men, about Galway, growing up there, the fields shouldering rocks and the rocks shouldering sunsets. 'It sounds lonely,' she said. He looked to the sun setting behind Saint Patrick's. 'Ireland's lonely, don't you think?' he said.

She consoled him about his girlfriend. 'Young women are randy,' she said. Anyway she suggested he might be better off without that girl and he knew what she was saying, hugging him to her domain of reckless iconoclasm. Still she had her pictures of Mary, her candles, her own image of purity. In the evenings without his girlfriend Desmond came here and the Liberties opened, an old rich part of Dublin. It opened in a song from a pub, the squeal of a pig from the abattoir, in the reflection of the sun on an ancient window.

But it was the song from the pub that most suggested this place, a widow's song, the song of a single woman, middle-aged but still spirited.

> An' what's that to anyone whether or no
> If I came to th' fore when she gave me th' cue?
> She clos'd her eyes tight as she murmur'd full low,
> Be good enough, dear, for to tie up my shoe.

He didn't bring Miles to the Rock of Cashel but he did bring him to the National Museum, to the National Gallery, to the Municipal Gallery. The school exploded with news of their relationship but Desmond didn't mind. It was too near the end of term and he definitely wasn't coming back.

70

Miles wasn't demanding. He said little. He was really his mother's child, a character's child, full of his own self-esteem. His mother definitely was a prostitute and Desmond appreciated that in her, her readiness to flaunt this country's disgusting double-standards and create not vice but a job by which she could surround herself with small luxuries. Miles had the curious air of one brought up on luxury. He ate cakes in Bewley's with ease.

They were planning to go further when bombs exploded in Dublin, killing thirty people, loyalist bombs. Desmond's girlfriend returned and rested on him; she was scared, he accepted her fright. Miles was forgotten. What was the meaning of this carnage; did it point to something? He looked to the blue Dublin sky outside. Yes, maybe to other places, other domains, a break with this country.

She spoke obsessively about Rilke and Goethe, the mystics, turning from violence to transformation. She wanted so much to escape pain. Her head rested on his chest. He could only go half-way to bringing her to a complete liberating mystical experience. It took a few weeks before he realized Miles wasn't going to school. He went looking for him, found him at home, his mother darning socks. Miles was reading a book of Irish legends. It was open at the tale of the Children of Lir. He looked at Desmond accusingly. Desmond had tea. Miles' mother was less friendly. What had Miles been telling her?

Desmond looked at Miles' book in his unease. He flicked through the story of the Children of Lir, young people turned into swans, destined to be swans until Christianity came to Ireland. But when the bells of Christianity sounded they shed their swans' apparel only to find they were no longer young and beautiful but old and shrivelled.

Always in Ireland there'd been bombs and violence, an attempt to break from inner violence. The spirit of Ireland forging itself like swans. But the violence inevitably reverberated on itself. The Dublin bombings had been but one

71

example, but looking into Miles' eyes now he saw a different interpretation of the Children of Lir; he saw that Miles knew he'd changed and that perhaps the last weeks had pushed him to a brink. He was about to leave the country. But if he went he'd never, ever come back to the same place. Miles' eyes were positively psychic, pent up, even a mischief in them. Desmond acknowledged that he'd understood.

'You've been reading about the Children of Lir?' he said to Miles.

'Yes, but some people never become swans,' Miles said, 'They're always ugly ducklings.' His mother laughed at that. 'Take me for example.' She played cards by herself. Desmond drank tea. Miles' eyes spoke a very urgent language, they articulated many questions, questions that ran too quickly to be counted. 'I'll see you soon,' Desmond said before leaving, 'Come back to school.' He told his girlfriend about Miles and she said that Miles was another hieroglyphic, the shadow of a possible child. She told Desmond that he was more Russian than Irish, that he'd always be misunderstood in his own country, by his own people. But if so, so would she. Her soul was already a swan in flight, an outward rush. She spoke of marriage, of children; he contracted her urgency. They both spoke of marriage. But in the space between them something was splintered. Miles walked again in the corridors of an ugly school, defining the space between them. He was neither child, nor adolescent, nor adult; a mixture of all these things, an intensely sensitive and knowledgeable youngster. He wore clothes that suggested a style years beyond his age. Sometimes he was a near caricature of *Vogue* magazine but always lovely, a mixture of male model and some young Irish adult who's just walked out of a confessional. Desmond's girlfriend took up the theme of flight. She looked to the sky as if it were possible to fly away; the theme was suddenly, in the aftermath of carnage, that of swans, restlessness spiralling to escape,

escape moulded into the artifact of steps, steps pacing towards undiscovered truths.

Desmond took Miles out in the evenings. They went to Gaj's Restaurant and Toners pub. Miles suddenly appeared very adult, no different from anyone else in Baggot Street.

Miles' mother was going out a lot. Desmond's girlfriend was staying in a lot, demanding attention. It was like looking in two different directions and he had to teach both people how to be swans.

His girlfriend said she'd like a child and Miles said he'd like a friend. 'We can't really be friends,' Desmond told him. 'There are too many years between us.'

Mrs. Gaj contemplated red carnations in her restaurant while a tin-whistle pierced the air outside. Miles suddenly looked at him. 'Do you want it?' he said.

Desmond knew what he was talking about, said nothing. The boy's shirt was melon pink that night. His fringe hazel. There was no reply from Desmond, a waiting from Miles, then a slinking away to Baggot Street bridge where swans on the canal could not be distinguished from empty cartons.

A friend died in the United States the following week, in New England in a car crash, and Desmond's girlfriend went there, never to come back. Desmond went to Europe. He returned some months later; worked in Ireland for some years in street theatre, then left Ireland maybe for good. On one of his first visits home he saw Miles outside Bartley Dunne's, Dublin's homosexual pub, in scarlet shirt and polka dotted tie. He didn't notice Desmond. Desmond recalled the fateful version of the Children of Lir, he also remembered a painting they'd seen in the National Gallery, a youngster, who looked like Miles and who also looked like a potential offspring of Desmond's, playing a tin-whistle. The swans had been counted, one by one, the Children of Lir, young people in H Blocks trying to get out of Ireland's misery, young people on the streets of Dublin picking their way out on punk music, but the child in the National

73

Gallery had not been accounted for, a young man who looked remarkably like Miles playing a tin-whistle. Some swans were gone, some people were trying to be swans, and maybe Desmond would be a swan who, like the Children of Lir, came back to find that he could never be what he was before, if it wasn't for the smile on Miles' face as he waited for the next customer.

The Irish in Love

Mrs. Hanratty's son had just been ordained a priest so there was a party. The whole village was invited and they came. There were cakes and scones and the traditional custard and jelly neatly set out on plates. There was sherry and port and Guinness and a lone fiddler played reels while a fat woman danced with the young priest, merging with him on the sitting-room floor. This was a small village, tucked into a corner of County Galway. The women of town most dominated the proceedings, done up to the hilt, in new dresses, dresses with patterns of Pacific waves or Australian birds on them. In fact everything just looked a little exotic tonight, the women, their perms, their dresses, their smiles and their eyes riveted to a fond image. It was Mrs. Hanratty herself who'd prepared the food. Now she was resting, smile on her face. She was the local librarian, husband dead. Her only son Gerald was suddenly ordained into the priesthood and as such took a most honoured place in his society. The only trouble was he was going away to South Africa. But she looked fulfilled, and she smiled despite the fact her son would be far from her and now there'd be just books. He was taking his place among the long line of Irish missionaries, bringing the faith to the dark people in the south African bush. No matter who she was talking to her eyes inevitably veered towards her son, the boy dancing in black.

Carmel O'Shaughnessy had come from Ballinasloe, herself the mother of two priests but she had one child killed in a motor accident and everyone knew that despite her orange and gleaming hair she was thinking of a son gone from her, her eyes emerald and shining but, behind the glow, full of sadness and the pain of loss.

There was no talk of loss tonight. People danced and drank and shuffled about with food. The Bishop arrived briefly, coming in, pausing· in various rapports with people. He went again almost unnoticed, leaving an impression of scarlet and a fat belly that discomfited the crowd. Here people were lean and purgatorial, but tonight the hollowness and the leanness was transformed. Eyes eagerly met eyes. Conversations were flowing and open and a variety of women who usually stayed at home in the hills with their buttermilk churns and their brown oak tables now flirted and floated about. Gerald himself sat alone after dancing with a variety of ladies. A young man, his forehead was already scarred by balding. His face was extremely young however. Mrs. O'Shaughnessy from Ballinasloe tasted Mrs. Hanratty's honey mousse with a fine teaspoon and declared it delicious as some other woman shrieked with laughter. It seemed to be a very funny thing that anyone should have pleasure for a change. Gerald was the hero of the night but he was temporarily forgotten as the festivities clouded the air. No one noticed his eyes, emerald eyes in his soft baby-like face, and how sad they were. A priest he was. A priest in the tradition of his people, leading the faithful. The first image he'd had of priests was of them leading the ordinary folk towards mountain rocks to celebrate mass in the penal days. It had been a persuasion of ultimate pain to him. Then there'd been a host of draconian uncles and grand uncles who'd been priests, ghosts in scrap-books, out there among the spiritually thirsty of the United States and Africa. There'd also been nuns who'd looked like robots. But it was his father dying of cancer that had settled him with this vocation, a sense of seeing things from a religious perspective. He'd gone to Maynooth, studied there, always a room which was haunted and locked up intriguing him. A dark

76

room wherein the forces of evil were supposed to be contained. No amount of masses would rid these forces, so they remained, young celibates having flung themselves from that window. Now only mice sidled within it. And unseen forces. Gerald knew those forces, forces of demonism and regret. He was a priest, a missionary priest going to South Africa to be among people as penalized and driven as the Irish during the penal laws. It was a neat measure. Fate would have it that a young Irish priest in the 1980s should go among the black people of South Africa. If he was a man of God he would honour his vocation and defy these screaming virgins. He'd be among the wretched.

Mrs. O'Shaughnessy grabbed him and urged him towards her blossoming bosom. He perceived her own sadness, regrets at having sent a child out for a tin of peas on a bicycle late on a winter's night once. He knew that she lived with the loss of her son moment by moment so as he danced with her he understood, understood the pain and meaning of absolute loss. He was leaving the world of the living, going into an unknown realm. The rest of his life he was married to God.

His mother was seated and she would be thinking of her husband, seven years gone now, of her many relatives, nuns, priests situated like lighthouses around the world, of her books. She'd be smiling at her triumph at pushing her only son into the priesthood, achieving the ultimate for him and saving him from the wiles of women. Yet with her too was sadness; maybe she was thinking of the boys who'd loved her once, who'd pinched her arms and roused her flesh. Gerald would never know the abandoned dream of another person's flesh. He'd never know the meteorite embraces, the meetings by a lake with the trees behind and the stars above, the whisper of Fairyland in the grass. Always there was talk of fairies in this neighbourhood, inspired by the lady who'd once lived in the local manor. Ghosts walked in this place and lovers were spellbound by draughts from another

77

country. But if Gerald would never know the abandon of the flesh he'd certainly encounter the reality of the spirit. With that thought Mrs. Hanratty would be comforting herself, smiling and sawing to the music. Her son danced with Mrs. O'Shaughnessy, her bosom ballasting his chest.

The women looked endearingly at him. The music was suddenly 'Slievenamban' — 'I never will forget the sweet maid that I once met in the valley of Slievenamban.' That reminded them of girlhood, of the crossroad dances, the carnival lights – twinkling one by one, orange and blue and red. Their faces lighted up now like those lights and they echoed the refrain. They had always been very modest procedures, these girlhood dances, but one or two of these women ceased to be maidens after these dances, felt the wet urgency of sex in the grass always inspired or threaded by dew. The virgins had been separated from those who weren't virgins, the chosen. Those who fell were rarely spoken to and had a kind of black mark on their faces. It was always known who'd made love.

Love-making was an opprobrium then; now all the women were fallen, old, wedded, mothers of many children. The children were gone or going from them. Gerald tonight encapsulated something that would remain with them by virtue of his chosen celibacy.

Celibacy to Gerald wasn't so much a vocation as a rite. For the moment he would be celibate in accordance with the rules. As a child he knew little of sex, wandering in the woods about his home he'd play with himself – everything there was moisture and growth, the thickening of moisture on a snail's back, the wet on the earth underneath an oak tree. His mother and his father had never seemed mutually attracted; a kind of penance in their relationship, as though they were sacrificing something every moment they were with one another. Then his father died. Gerald faced adulthood. He'd been a lean gangly adolescent, a star on the local hurling field. Religion attracted him. He could now see he'd been pushed into it by his mother. But still he'd felt the need to drape his lean body in black. In Maynooth there'd been boys who'd attracted him, who'd attracted one another. There'd always been a woman on the horizon. He'd never slept with anyone. But maybe in Africa he'd meet some robust Swedish doctor, far from Ireland, and sleep with her and plug his tongue into her rich femininity. Perhaps different laws operated among the snakes, the antelopes, the rainbow birds than here among woods and squirrels and otters. Even as he contemplated thighs and bushes of auburn pubic hair a woman grabbed him and he was compelled to dance, an old time waltz, going through a routine again, a slow waltz on a floor to music of an accordion and a fiddle now.

The proceedings were interrupted when Jimmy Moran, the local story-teller, - the seanchaí - arrived, parking his brown bicycle outside, taking off his cap as he entered, seating himself, greeting all within, taking a glass of Guinness and launching into tales of the past. Jimmy was one of the last of the old story-tellers, a gardener on the local estate until the lady of the manor died. His presence was compulsory at weddings and wakes. He'd made a vocation out of story-telling, tying the threads of the past together. He launched into a tale now of an archbishop who'd sailed to Canada in 1902 and saw a shoal of whales along the way. He then proceeded with stories about Gerald's relatives, priests who'd distributed themselves widely, their school-days, adventures in the locale. The time Father Tony fell into quicksand and began sinking and was saved when a pig approached and he caught the pig's feet. The time Father Martin climbed a tree in the local estate and wouldn't come down for days. Daft tales. And then talk inevitably led to tales of the past, Lord Clonricarde who lived nearby, the felling of woods, the silencing of mass bells in Ireland, the Wild Geese, young men in Galway departing with wolf-hounds, duels in Austria among the emigrant Irish, prison sentences in later days of Irish people in Tasmania. The rich persona of Irish history emerging, the galaxy of colours on a skeleton's shawl.

Jimmy's triumph was for suggesting hope where everybody knew there was despair, hope by virtue of an embroidery of portentous events on an otherwise desolate history. He made it sound romantic and maybe it was romantic, the squeal of a bagpipe across the years, a bagpipe leading the native Irish from Ireland, the remonstrance of an emotion that although gone would return. 'In 1689 the magpies came to Ireland,' Jimmy said, 'and it was said that the British would never leave Ireland until the magpies went.' Mrs. Hawthorne had just died. She was the last of the British around here. So Jimmy took up her tale, the ghost-like beautiful spinster who'd written fairy-tales and grown a wide variety of starry-eyed anemones.

An accordion played again, slower, sadder music. People were mesmerised, images of the Jacobeans fleeing Aughrim, images of the Irish departing from the Limerick, the Wild Geese, images of the native poets forging on, subversives in the hold of a ship, in the dark of a bog, on the wet of a mountain, carrying on a tradition that spliced Ovid with native history. And then there was the bagpipe, the bagpipe that had led the Irish into exile from Galway in 1652, from Limerick in 1691, diffusing them in Flanders and Austria and Hungary, a nation of men dispersed among the armies of Europe, resolutely remembering the songs of Ireland, the music of Ireland, the harpists, the poets, the pipers. The might of a fire in a big house. 'We are a nation of hosts,' Jimmy said to Mrs. Hanratty. Women sat on a bench like birds in autumn, eyes alive and waiting. Jimmy had a gift. Jimmy uplifted and transformed things, ashes into embryo of flames, a young priest's ordination into a step of history. Gerald he said was going out to be a spiritual hero. He would heal the sick and feed the hungry. Gerald, hurler and scholar, had hit the bull's-eye of his people. He was reckoning with the forces of history, a history which had tried to expurgate their religion but which had failed because their faith was as flames, seeming to die and exploding again, rife with strength and defiance. Above him was a picture of John Paul, blessing the Irish in Galway, evidence indeed of something kindled a long time ago which no amount of attack had abated. Gerald sat, an inheritor of all these, folk stories, adventure stories, tales of spiritual defiance and triumph. Among the fields, the trees, the stone walls another Irish priest was forged like a face on the old monastery walls of Ireland. His mother glowed with pride. Gerald smiled. Jimmy humoured him. Strange the tragic comparison with penal Ireland for that's how he saw himself, someone going to the hills to lead the hungry. His flight to South Africa was a partaking in an old combat, that between oppressor and oppressed. There was music again, fiddle music. No one danced but they listened to a lament, a lament for those gone into exile, for those who died of famine, for those fallen in war. More than anything for the lost sense of love among the Irish, the big house, the glowing flames, the roast on the spit, the visiting musicians, the ease of a civilization all but exterminated in the seventeeth century but clinging in a note of music, in a story-teller's voice, in a priest's blessing.

The accordionist joined the fiddler and stiff bodies rose to dance. Mrs. O'Shaughnessy was weeping now for her lost child and Mrs. Hanratty was staring, staring into the moon, knowing she'd driven her child to this isolation and regretting it.

Out in the moonlight Gerald stood. He wanted so much to believe what he was doing was right. But it was just in order, a step in a line of many steps. He was taking no plunge maybe but committing himself to the absolute. 'If thy sins be as scarlet, they shall be made as white as snow'.

The moon looked down on him and he hoped his sores would be healed, his doubts, his negations, his unease with this garb. He hoped he'd create from it and so be able to shed it one day and appear as what he should be, an ordinary person. But before his catalogue of despair became too intense a laughing woman took hold of him and kissed him and wished him well before she took off into the night.

Jimmy Moran drank whiskey, elfishly, defiantly. Mrs. O'Shaughnessy wept, tears on her red face under her orange hair. Mrs. Hanratty was silent as a woman saying a rosary to herself. An old man entered, the local would-be writer, and shouted about his novels, the ones never written but much imagined, then left when no one listened, going off to talk to his fallen golfing friends in the night.

Gerald was to leave on Saturday. People sang 'For he's a jolly good fellow'. Mrs. Hanratty forgot her doubts and lighted up.

No one noticed Jimmy Moran take his bicycle and cycle off into the night, leaving people not with remembrance of tales of duels in 1780 or the Wild Geese in 1692 but of tales of red-haired women far away and long ago, women who were varicose and cancerous now, some still with red and gleaming hair but all with sadness, with a backlog of memories of dead children, still-born children, children in exile who never wrote, children in despair, children on the verge of flight, husbands in mental agony. But the music of 'Slievenamban' rushed to their consolation and lights spark-led again, coloured lights on country roads long ago and figures moved in for the final waltz, the Mary Annes and the Susan Marys, big bottoms, lovely dresses, feet moving precisely to the music as if this had been ordained, a rythmn, a series of steps, a long time ago and all they could do was obey as Gerald obeyed his call to foreign parts and outlying stars.

Time of Betrayal

Coming into Dublin was a balletic motion, arriving on a sunny day, the mountains of his childhood below, china blue. He identified an island, then another island. Suddenly the plane was over a housing estate and the rushing emerald of Ireland. He was about to land.

Everything Damian saw now in terms of dance: walking, seeing, rising in the morning. Since going to Brussels his perceptions had changed and engaged the things about him in a new tempo. Life had become crystal, life had become refined.

Walking down Grafton Street on a May day Damian Curly passed a bookshop which had just closed down, its windows like a mortuary, brown paper over the glass at odd intervals and elsewhere a sight of a desolate area, the books gone, the shelves empty.

Bewley's was like a steam engine, it suddenly engaged you in odours, steaming up, enticing. How could you resist the sharpness of coffee, the acerbic weight of scent and the sharpness of distilling coffee cutting through the air? Within a stained glass window; coffee by yourself. His aunt used take him here as his mother used always to be too engaged with priests or nuns. Aunt Delia would bring him here, a child in a blue coat, hoist him on a chair, light stretching through the stained glass window. When the sun was shining it created an illusion of the miraculous, Dublin in the late fifties and early sixties badly needing the miraculous. One bathed in the light of excitement.

Damian was home for a week, a young dancer working in Europe. It was his first time home since his father's death. He wasn't going to stay with his mother though. He was going to stay with his ex-wife.

Married at twenty-two, divorced at twenty-four, now twenty-nine going on thirty, an exile, a stranger possibly in his own country. He examined his bun for cherries. They leapt at him, scarlet. Recognising the cherries in Bewley's buns was recognising you were back.

Outside it had begun to rain, a penalty for Grafton Street. The rain beat, stiffly. Damian walked along, rain on his face, rain on the statues outside Trinity, rain hastening the flutter of the tricolour over the GPO.

His father took him many times to the Easter commemoration parade here, guns, tanks, the paucity of the Irish army. Always the widows of heroes in the rain, looking anxious, and bishops, in maroon.

The Archbishop of Dublin had confirmed him, a thin wizened man whose eyes emanated extreme distrust and who handled even little boys with opprobrium. Damian looked into the sky; cloud was breaking. Again it was one of Aunt Delia's miraculous moments, light breaking in the sky.

Grace was living with someone and was obviously pregnant. That was the shock. That she was living with someone who ran a vegetable store he knew. Her pregnancy though was shocking and wounding, a physical confrontation. She greeted him blandly, like many Irish people involved in the arts. Grace lived with Pete in a new house in the North side. She'd abandoned the South side, rich part of Dublin, had adopted the North side like sackcloth. Time to be rough and ready, time to be proletarian and self-denying. Pete stood beside her at dinner that evening; together a tableau they kept vigilance, wondering what he would introduce to their world that would threaten it.

He'd met Grace at college, children of the Dublin middle classes. They'd formed a liaison, his first; perfumes of

84

marijuana exhaled around them, the philosophy of Hermann Hesse and Jung, inklings of Erich Fromm. One searched for love on the thin sustenance of one's parents' money. He'd been attracted to Grace because of her philosophy of hope, her love of old men with white beards, Martin Buber, Monet, Tolstoy. Her room had been adorned with photographs of reclining white bearded men, men in the golden state of their old age, men in ramshackle suits and sun-hats always with a glow in their cheeks and a smile which kept all at bay, life, its many contradictions.

Grace had had a lovely smile. She'd been delicate, porcelain, a waif who'd slithered through Dublin at sixteen, a kind of whore at seventeen, taking heroin. It was usual, girls in blue jeans who rushed out of doors in Dublin's South side. College had tempered her. They'd belonged to the dope scene. She had been an expert in marijuana, knew the nationalities of every shade of it. Grace had led him from virginity, the half-orphaned state he'd lived in at home. Pagodas by the sea, railway tracks which swept along the tide, the miserable sea-gulls of Sandymount Strand, all these things were exhumed and halted in his love-making with Grace; boys in blue blazers, Dublin, the life of it.

They'd married when they finished college, more to have a wedding than anything else. His mother wept. Lots of young people in bright clothes were present. Grace wore a pink dress which displayed a maximum of skin. She clung to peonies. Afterwards he'd reflected Grace had loved dressing him up. As though he were a doll. He wore a suit, wide collared white shirt, hair cut for £8.95. Afterwards they had a reception in Grace's home, marijuana smuggled into lavatories, a variety of singers crooning about love and nervous breakdowns. They spent a weekend honeymoon in Glencree, County Wicklow, bringing a friend. But Grace was anxious for Grafton Street, the street she once lifted young boys off, bringing them into backrooms when rough sex was popular among the girls of Dublin's South side.

85

She needed the thrill of dope, of squandering your life, talking to jewellers and street artists. That's possibly the only moment when he loved Grace, when he saw her interviewing young craftsmen and street merchants blown in from the West of Ireland, asking them about gullies in Mayo or Galway. They'd always deigned to live in the West, but they never made it. Damian taught in a vocational school, Grace did a course for teaching the blind.

Then one day bombs ripped through Dublin, three of them. They'd been due to meet in Grafton Street that day; Grace had been rushing along when she'd witnessed the worst of the explosions, Damian had come upon the one in Nassau Street, a lesser calamity, a few bodies, an uncertain gathering of spectators. That finished them. The North of Ireland was fine on paper but when it came and strangled young life in Dublin they fled. They went to Mexico for the summer, sleeping on beaches, forgetting nuns, priests, dope-vendors, trees in Stephen's Green, the ducks, the gulls, the pubs, the tin-whistle playing, the keen of a Gaelic singer in a pub.

They marched on, up the west coast of Mexico. Grace was pregnant. Grace lost the filament of her child in autumn. The ikon broke, ikon of illusion. They'd never really loved one another, had an ephemeral relationship with the trees on Stephen's Green yes, but they'd never really known one another. In Los Angeles in the autumn they'd smoked dope, uplifted themselves on cocaine, heroin. Grace had been dabbling, primal therapy, Zen buddhism, Eskimo art. Los Angeles had baked, then the cold came in November, a nervous Pacific draught. The surfers were gone, the beaches empty, those mesmeric people who rose at evening on the waves when the sun had concentrated into an orange unyielding ball, coming, bodies on the breakers like a lost tribe no longer to be seen, expiated like an illusion.

Grace flew back to Dublin with the punctuality of a migratory bird. Damian stayed, digging into the last reefers.

His marriage had broken. The only relationship he'd ever had with a girl was over.

He too returned to Dublin, but briefly. Dublin was cold, Dublin was anxious, oil had gone up in price, smiles were fewer, the children of Grafton Street gone into a sleep. Maybe some day a prince would come and kiss them into wakefulness. Damian didn't wait for the intimacy of this act, those lips that would revive life again and resuscitate a drowning generation. He left Ireland, on a plane, attended a dance and mime school in London, this the sum total of his Irish experience, an unborn child, a shadow on the womb, an indeterminate foetus that never made it but tried, really tried.

That night they went drinking, Grace, Pete, Damian, at first in Grafton Street, the Bailey, Neary's, a stint in the Shelbourne Bar, a woman playing a fossilized version of 'The Mountains of Mourne' on the piano, then Baggot Street, Doheny & Nesbitt's. Grace had dyed her hair henna; she'd lost nothing of her porcelain build. In fact her features had sharpened, more frightened. He remembered her softer, more assured. She worked as a stage manager now, opting for the theatre. Her pregnancy was like a convenience, a sustenance against time. When it left her would she shrivel into inconstancy and uncertainty? Her mood now suggested imminent change, a high water mark, change one way or another. She demanded gins and tonics, he had white wine. Pete drank Guinness, Pete verging on the mythical proletarian they'd all yearned for, not quite there. He came from a humbler part of the South side, Dolphin's Barn, had the imagination and the enterprise to make capitalism out of green peas and cabbages. During the days Grace worked in the shop, at night she bordered on the stage.

Everywhere they went Grace and Pete recognised and spoke to people. Dublin is a city where you know everybody or nobody. Damian was verging on the nobody stage, not quite there, one or two gracious solicitors remembering him.

He loved this street, Baggot Street, Gaj's Restaurant, now having changed hands, Doheny & Nesbitt's with its Victorian apparel and its turnover of solicitors. Most of all he loved the street. His favourite tin-whistle player had committed suicide, but she walked, the red-headed theatre manager in black who always drank alone and pressed her secrets to herself, integrity in a city which tears your insides out as though you were a stuffed teddy-bear or an abandoned rag doll.

Grace smiled at his jokes. Pete was cautious. Damian spoke of Brussels. His flat. Rue de la Senne. The plays they produced, based on *Great Expectations* or *Wuthering Heights* with mime and dance. He'd played the young lover in *Le Rouge et le Noir* and that baffled Grace. She didn't wish to see him as lover. The world outside Dublin was moribund and he was part of it.

They walked home. Scare stories could be heard everywhere of vandalism but young skin-heads smiled at Damian and he smiled back.

Next morning he went to see his mother. He had a horror of her. Last time he'd seen her was when his father had died. She lived in the house looking towards the sea, with her warped collection of clerical mementoes, pictures of priests in Ghana or Nigeria, her many cousins, nuns in Mexico, all draconian, all unforgiving, all relentlessly dedicated to the ensnaring of souls, catching them like the Bible says with hooks rather than prayers. Her immediate litany, as he expected, was one of sadness. She had reserved it for him, her suffering. She was lonely, desperately lonely, yet he knew his parents had never got on and his most lasting memory from childhood was of his father, half naked, holding him against a starchy chest, crying, crying because of the unflinching and binding negativity of his mother. His father had been a civil servant, in childhood in a chestnut suit, later in grey; a wise man, a prayerful man. He went to mass in Sandymount church but he'd also banqueted with

88

the clever and inebriated men of Dublin. He'd taught Damian this, to look on the underside of things, to halt before making judgements. His mother by comparison was like the Spanish Inquisition, always searching for odium and waiting to pull people up over it. She'd lived the last months in loneliness. Her Christmas had been destitute. The days were long without Con. The weather was foul. All her clerical friends stared out of photographs to confirm this view. And he, what was he up to? Brussels, so far away. The theatre, mime, dance, scatter-brained illusions. Couldn't he return to Dublin, go back to college, do an M.A.? Her eyes twinkled though when she spoke of Brussels. She'd gone there with her husband once, to Brussels and Paris after the war. They'd had a great time. Other than visiting a church in the Rue du Bac in Paris where the miraculous medal had been handed from Our Lady to an unsuspecting nun there'd been no religious excursions, a few cathedrals may-be but even they looked depraved. Secretly Damian sup-posed an approval on his mother's face, not for dance or mime but for the idea of Europe, Catholic Europe, the sal-vation of Irish people during the penal laws. Her son was dancing now, he was a bohemian and even the word re-vived music, the seductive paths of youth. As gulls dipped outside the curtains Mrs. Curly knew that in some way her son had changed residence, not just from Dub-lin to Brussels, but he'd altered context, Ireland to a world outside, the world of possibilities she and her hus-band had explored for a few days, a labyrinth after the war.

They had whiskey together and she became merry and melancholy in turn and Damian felt like doing what his father had done years ago to him, taking her frail frame in his arms, but even as he considered that some cloud around her resisted him, a sudden dark cloud, the piercing coldness, the sense of having been humiliated. Off she was again about loneliness and destitution, aiming her remarks at him, cold-blooded comments about being left alone. Damian left. Rain came for a split second. Then sunshine.

Damian would be back for tea the following day.

He spent his afternoon in Bewley's, a grotto beside the stained glass. He anxiously handled a cup. The cup for those moments was a crystal ball. Neither his mother nor Grace really knew of his present life, creativity yes, uncertainty, but also wine in the Flemish part of Brussels, talking to young labourers from Flanders. There was a beat to Brussels, the confused rhythms of many tongues, pop music gargled from juke-boxes, no time reserved for tomorrow. Tomorrow didn't exist, an unborn child. Today people danced, sang, composed poetry, plays. The nuclear bomb was coming, the Russians were insinuating themselves across the world. The egg of pleasure continually cracked, spewing its contents over the momentary gleam of a Moroccan immigrant on a dance floor or the cautious smile of a Flemish labourer in a café.

And yet his life wasn't dissolute. He made a collage, plays with his company. That more than anything was what he couldn't reveal to Grace. His friends now were like a third sex, neither male nor female, neither gay in the way people in Dublin advertised themselves but somehow different, a cross between genders, dissolute in that way. They reminded him of a sonorous statement from Sandymount church; leave father and mother, sisters and brothers and come follow me. He'd left father and mother, sisters and brothers, concepts of gender and followed the momentary, the flashing, that which yielded nothing concrete but a mime, a dance, a festive piece on a floor in Brussels, celebrating the ephemeral, celebrating the occasional joys of life, celebrating the lasting pleasures of communication and art.

They dined out that evening, Grace, Pete, himself. In a new restaurant in Dublin, downstairs. The wine was good. The food was adventurous. Grace was dressed in black, ready for a kill. Pete spoke of vegetables with great sincerity, then of school in Dolphin's Barn, the brothers with their canes, the brother who tried to drown himself in the Grand Canal but found the water too shallow and was found wading there, cane still in hand.

It was Damian who ordered the second bottle of wine and it was only then that Damian realized Pete resented him; that Grace's store of memories of their marriage was maybe more flourishing than he'd realized, the trip up the Mexican coast, the Californian surfers, the marmalade sunsets. And then he recreated his love for her and felt tender towards the child in her womb, wondering what had become of their love, why it had perished. But even it seemed a museum piece to him, he could only work up a remote enthusiasm for it and then all seemed doomed to him, this city, the hotels, the many items in the museum, but she smiled, against her present lot she smiled a Trojan smile and he felt like grabbing her and making off with her, but Pete stared into his face and he knew that Pete realized what he was thinking, having come around to it in some odd circuitous way.

Before going to bed, Damian lying on a mattress, Pete came into his room, shirt off, chest naked, and was oddly solicitous, talking of his vegetables, the Dublin mountains, warming to Damian's artistic career. He knew Pete was confused by certain elements of Grace but didn't want to say it. Damian could have told him, Grace was a spoilt avaricious child at worst, at best a creative angel. But was there creativity wanting in her now, her blue eyes blank, her features poised like daggers? Had this city, the rain got into her? Before he slept Damian prayed for her, an odd idle childish prayer. There was something of her he still possessed, the space in her womb from which their child vanished.

Next afternoon he went to see his mother. She was in a pretty pink dress, her hair was permed. He brought her a plant. She'd made scones and piled cream and cherry jam on them.

'Auntie Sarah's moving to Florida'. A nun leaving a convent in Saint Paul, Minneapolis. 'Uncle Fred is going on a cruise.'

She spoke of aunts and uncles, lacerated Gay Byrne, Irish television compère, for some item he'd had on the all persuasive *Late Late Show*. The sea beamed. Howth danced in the distance. He asked her if she'd like to come to Nice with him some time and she behaved as though she'd been kissed for the first time.

Have a romance with his mother. What better?

She warned him against the Charismatic Movement as though he were in danger of joining it in Brussels, and then she was off again about priests and nuns. He would have quelled her but here his ikons were strong, a child in a blue blazer at school, a boy naked in Blackrock baths' changing-room, an adolescent going to University College, Belfield, picking his way down uniform corridors, his brain washed by the syndromes of Thomistic philosophy and Hegelian metaphysics.

Grace had seduced him in the flat of a friend, virgin boy, boy with thoughts of far flung Catholic philosophers and the buttocks of other boys. He'd missed male companionship in adolescence; all his life adolescence would recycle, a yearning. His father had taken him on his naked breast once and he'd wanted to take other people on his own breast, nurture them against the cyclones of priests and the cataclysm of despair which warped his parents' marriage.

His mother was fecund today, his mother was talkative. He talked back, resolving her loneliness a little, and he saw her as she made tea, a misplaced nun. Her husband had violated her and she had tormented his earnest solitude, his prayerful journeys around Dublin, his absolute openness, to priest or to profligate.

The sun came out more strongly. He forgave her, forgave Irish catholicism, its warping influence, its secrets of despair.

92

He went out that night in Dublin by himself and had a great time, sat in pubs, talked to people as his father would have done, a student from Nigeria, a youth from Ballyfermot, a Divine Light missionary. He had chips, golden and crusty, in the Coffee Inn and an inspired glass of red wine. He celebrated Dublin. 'Mr. Tambourine Man' played. Pictures of Rome stood about, the eternal city. The wine was bitter and yet refreshing. His eyes searched a street, a city. He knew how he loved this city; he'd come back again and again. He adored the gulls, revered the rain, wallowed in the cold, but most of all loved the spaces between crumbling houses, old trees, canal walks, spaces to be alone.

Grace was peculiarly cool when he returned. She was sitting with Pete. He tried to communicate his enthusiasm to her. She looked at him with a famished stare. 'Meet any young boys?' And he knew she was talking of the time she'd caught him sleeping with a boy in Los Angeles.

Why this city which always must return to the barbarous point? 'Is it my fault?' he thought, 'Is it something in me? Have I done wrong? What did I do to Grace, to my mother, to Pete? Why always the hurts, the abuse, the humiliation? Why does everything shrivel here? What is it about this town that sends its children away with a thirst for revenge or with sores that go way beneath the skin and will always linger if the miraculous doesn't dissolve them?'

He walked into the night. No skin-heads attacked him. He walked to the Green and greeted a country garda. He walked to Rathmines and back. Dawn came, picking at the sky, birds chirping. 'My name is Damian Curly,' he told himself, 'I'm twenty-nine, going on thirty, changing states of being, changing cities, changing lives.'

Few people stirred in Dublin but he encompassed all of it, the eyesores, the visionary Georgian doors, the antique windows. He'd grown up here, been schooled here, sexually longed here, made love here, married here.

The fungus of his marriage had been the fungus of his life, bound to fail, born on a false premise; that the affluent have special privileges. He wanted for Grace's sake to go back over it all again, to analyse, reinterpret but he realized the foolishness of this, that one can't go back, that one must leave the dead to bury the dead.

His father lay in Dean's Grange. His mother was stored into sleep by relics. His former wife slept with another man. He talked briefly to a tramp, stared into travel-shop windows, was briefly accosted by a stranger. He wanted to coin a single image that would unite multiple abortions but couldn't, found himself with a train of memories, memories that wouldn't budge.

At thirteen he encountered Brendan Behan's funeral in this city. His Aunt Delia had clutched his hand. The funeral had wound past bins and bridges, something merciless about it. People had stopped, harkened, a bard dead, a city grieving. Later, much later, long after Aunt Delia had died of cancer, that image had stayed with him and if he could select anything it was that, Brendan Behan's funeral train, a long winding cortège, absorbing all that came after, Blackrock baths, school, marriage, the rain, the mountains, a momentum leading towards exile and an exile always pivoting on the point of return. He remembered the sense of shame which had made people tremor when Brendan Behan had died. He remembered his aunt's hand, cold, gripping his. He remembered the silence and yet the relief, relief that this country had once again yielded genius and even if he was dead at least one could wallow in the aftermath.

There'd been other funerals since, his aunt's, his father's, but none so chilling as that on a faroff Saturday in childhood. He wanted to rush home, tell Grace what he had just thought, that maybe it hadn't been their fault, the breakdown of their marriage, that maybe it wasn't her fault that she needed to hurt him, that maybe all was predestined in a

94

child's precocious vision, but even as he thought to hurry, another child passed him, this time a tinker child, shuffling along, wrapped in a coloured shawl, hair gold, eyes gleaming and a smile on her face that made you forget all, father and mother, sisters and brothers, as it followed its way into the dawn of Grafton Street.

A Fancy Dress Party

It was the last day of the circus. Madame López, clairvoyant, sang an aria across the fair Green, a crocodile wriggled
its tail and a child, one of the last children in the world,
looked on. The circus was closing down, a modest circus
that came every year with a lion, a crocodile, a weight-lifter
who also improvised as lion tamer, a clown, an opera singer
and a young acrobat cum dancer. The caravans were painted
bright as usual, the sun shone, the Protestant church stood
out as if nothing had changed, but an anchor weighed down
the hearts of the circus folk. It was the end.

A pilgrimage of coloured lights stood out that night,
orange lights, blue lights against the Ballinasloe night. The
clown blew a bugle. Madame López sang from *Madame
Butterfly*, her aria sounding over the Green, compelling all
into stillness. A young acrobat danced and cycled on a
tightrope. The weight-lifter hoisted massive weights. The
lion made a bow and someone scrambled in dressed as a
gorilla. The crocodile peeped in, grunted, grumbled about
something and hastily retreated.

Some nuns sat in the audience, a scattering of children,
middle-aged couples, one or two delinquent boys. It wasn't
just that there had been a fall in the numbers who attended
the circus; their audiences had been snatched away and what
remained was a mirror of themselves, the lonely, the soulful.
Mick O'Connor, proprietor, continually pointed out he was
a star once, but Madame Lopez only sang, Puccini, Rossini,
debasing his every statement. She could have been in La

Scala, she often muttered, but no one listened to her either, and she'd stare at a paper carnation with her jade eyes.

It was May. There were few stars. The stillness and freshness of foliage penetrated the tent. It was Tim O'Mahony the clown who stole the show, gallivanting and jumping, exuding jokes that weren't really jokes but poeticised jests. He had a gift of language, a man from Connemara with a Russian sailor father, a strong man, a boy even, with eyes that sparkled and changed like the sea, from glee to an abiding pain. Now that the circus was closing he was sailing away like his father, to Mexico, to Peru, seeking a golden fleece.

Few people in the circus had energy to stretch. Madame López was taking up palmistry in Bray, near Dublin. The Czechoslovak weight-lifter was going to work on construction in Dublin. The lion and the crocodile were already purchased by another circus and Mick, Mick was going into retirement, going to live with his sister on an estate in Liverpool. Only Trina the acrobat and Tim the clown seemed to have energy left. Trina was young and Tim was full of excitement, except that his excitement was motivated not by things seen but by the undercurrent of things, the bottom of the sea, the depth of the emotions, a realm guessed, conjured, never touched. Finally it was these two who would leave here and go on to other things. Everybody else seemed embodied in Madame López's crystal ball, a travesty of their own intentions.

Madame López, forever dressed in black, had had good days. She'd seen the rising tide of circus life, the drift-weed. She'd entertained, sung, danced sevillanas, roused a Spanish chorus wherever she went with her beauty. Now her beauty was spent and she was retiring over a fish and chip shop in Bray. She had no complaints, no ill-will towards anyone. Jan, the Czechoslovak, had lost his wife while fleeing from Czechoslovakia after the Russian invasion. He'd literally lost her. On a road in August. He'd gone in for white wine in a

97

café shouldering a jar of marigolds. She'd disappeared on a road through a rye field. Later he discovered she was living with another man in Prague but it was too late; he'd gone to Ireland and Mick O'Connor's primitive circus, the only place where he could be employed. So he heaved and lifted weights and tried to forget a feckless wife who lay down with another man in a field of rye when they were fleeing politics.

Mick O'Connor himself was a tall order to take, a long agonized man, face full of frailty, elbows jaunty. He'd had a long life in show business now. Show business had disowned him. He'd been of a good East Galway family, ran away to England, got a job in a circus, returned to Ireland, acted little parts in Shakespeare like elves and wolves and devils, opened his own show combining Shakespeare with the optics of the circus, travelled Ireland, was besieged by nuns. Now the nuns watched television. They no longer needed Mick O'Connor.

Trina shouldn't have had so much abundance. Her family were Jewish, Dublin Jews and her grandfather had died in Belsen. She'd given the circus much trouble, her mind and soul like broken glass. Often she'd wake up screaming in the night, crying that someone had pulled the hair out of her doll. Her mother had arrived in Dublin from Europe and she had surrendered her daughter to the circus at an early age, but Trina remembered a father who'd left her, always startled as though he'd touched electricity. She remembered the pain and the doubts that had driven her family from Paris through London to Dublin. Her mother and her father had the circus in their blood, they also being performers but all they could do now was drain bottles of alcohol, her father in Glasgow now, her mother in Dublin, the pain always there, Belsen, Dachau; mid-European Jews who'd nearly been exterminated. Trina was fresh and gay as daisies now but once they'd visited her in Ballinasloe mental hospital, Madame López with carnations, this time real and all the

98

toothless patients stood back and grinned as Madame sang from *Aida*.

She was better now, twenty-one, going back to Dublin, reneguing on acrobatics, studying typing. Her mother had it planned for her. Tim O'Mahony too was a lively one. He had Russian and Irish forebears, was muscular and had green eyes, full of brightness, with a swiftness that urged towards vision. He spoke of quest and absorbed Trina in his imaginings. He was bent on seeking the sun.

Tim mesmerised the crowd as clown. Trina floated like a dove. Mick appeared like a sexual fetishist in boots with white trousers. Madame López did a wobbly sevillana and Jan drove a lion around like a heifer.

The crowd were silent waiting for more. So Madame López sang her favourite song 'We'll go no more aroving' in faltering tenor voice. The lion growled in melancholy approval. An adult looking child looked at his watch and nuns made off. Mick O'Connor wanted to stop them and ask for something, a bouquet, but no bouquets were flowing, televisions shattering the vibrations of Ballinasloe, bellowing televisions and moribund minds.

In this Green he'd risen to the heights of Othello and Iago, playing both. He'd urged rousing performances as murderers, rapists, adulterers. He'd shocked and inspired and if that wasn't good enough he wed a trail of animals to a virtuous performance of Shakespeare and Victorian imitators of Shakespeare. He'd spellbind with a few rags thrown together in a magical way. His mother always said he'd come to no good, herself a Free Stater who'd produced a train of insipid solicitors. He'd been the wild one, gone to England in the thirties, stowed away in a circus, ridden the vans, fed the lions, acted the clown outside the performance area, beguiled all he met, won credentials to return to Ireland and join a travelling theatre group who were never sure what they were, fancy dress party, serious actors, paupers. They'd travelled the length and breadth of Ireland, Kerry, Antrim.

The sea most seduced. People were more gullible by the sea. They'd crossed to Aran and frightened the islanders with a rendition of *Macbeth*, all of them dressed like draconian reverend mothers. They'd performed *A Midsummer Night's Dream* in the open on Dun Aengus, a fort in Aran, jumping about the rocks like lunatics bred from the Irish soil. Then fate had changed its course; monkeys, snakes, lions came, the nature of Mick's group changed and he started one of his own, combining these elements, high drama with the growls and ferocious appetities of lions. They'd sailed to islands, bringing jungle beasts. A snake once escaped on an island off Donegal and the priest found him and blessed him, Saint Patrick walking again. In latter days though Mick had settled down to this, a collection of ragamuffins, the very old, the young, a lion who complained a lot, a particularly vicious crocodile. The tail had long been wagging out of his world.

The show over, lights off, it was time to mourn. The bottles were in order; Madame López had more plastic flowers than usual and the Sacred Heart was pointing to his heart above this extravaganza as though waiting for attention too. The circus folk assembled. Like the faithful shuffling in for confession in a rural church. Tim. Jan. Trina. Mick. And Madame López waiting there, shawl around her, no crystal ball in sight but a table full of flowers and bottles of wine as though it could be there, hidden in the mélange. People chattered, a budgie sang. Wine was consumed. Outside the fair Green surrounded them like a sea.

Madame López spoke of Spain, her youth there, Andalusia, the gipsies, the flamenco guitars, the caravan trails to the sea; the waiting grotesques of civil war. She'd left Spain before the war, travelled to London, opened a clairvoyant's corner in Covent Garden, then inspired by the opera house sang in a circus. The circus toured England and Ireland; in Belfast she met an ex-parson who'd joined the circus, married him, stayed in Ireland, had children, then relinquished home and settlement for a latter day circus, Mick

100

O'Connor's. Her daughter owned a fish and chip shop in Bray and it was to there she was retiring, but her circuitous eyes held this, the armament of the past, whine of a flamenco song, azure spray of the sea. She had this authenticity, Spain on the perimeter of time. And she did not claim second sight in vain. She had a Spaniard's inbuilt distrust and yet a wildness, an intoxication that disturbed her late at night and compelled her into a sevillana, a budgie watching.

Jan drowsed over drink. There was a future as a construction worker. Already he was advertising in the lonely heart columns of magazines, looking for a wife. Hopefully there would be a new wife somewhere in the world for him. His own wife would burn in Hell he vowed, a whore. The Russians came but all she thought of was men. Ireland being a chaste country he hoped his wife would be chaste. Madame López nodded benignly. He'd meet a good woman. He deserved one, and off she was again about Spanish women, if they committed adultery their knuckles would be smashed. Jan nodded approvingly. One look at Madame López one saw the jade of her eyes had darkened again and it was again Andalusia, storm clouds growing. One look at Jan told you his eyes were smashed by pain; there were tanks rumbling through Prague again, marigolds in vases, white wine on the pub table and the heat of August splintered in the trees on Wenceslas Square.

Trina made to calm him but he rebuffed her touch and snorted. He'd become a good Catholic and suspected this girl of immoral behaviour. Mick launched into one of his perennial reminiscences. 'We died, we grow older,' Madame López lamented but the faces of Trina and Tim were young, she shining, he with golden skin, brave eyes, dark hair, flecked with blond and always boldness in his eyes if they were happy or sad.

Trina had been borne off by young men on motorbikes recently, she'd left her series of mental hospitals behind. Her face anticipated the city now. Her mother would be drinking

101

wine but she'd meet nice boys, would go to discothèques and cinemas. The girl who danced in a cream costume would stop dancing. She'd start living.

Tim's eyes were intense now, more intense than Irish, Russian, bearing his father in his mind, Russian sailor who'd stopped off in Galway and impregnated a woman from Inishbofin. Tim's Irish uncle had been in the circus and he'd followed him.

Now he discoursed on Plato; he told the party life was a fight between the mind and the soul. If so someone had pulled a trigger and renewed the fight because now tears, drunkenness, laughter, reminiscences, patience, shame came in turn.

Tim played a fiddle. Madame López sang 'Moonlight in Picardy' and Mick launched into 'My Singing Bird'. Only Jan drank on, he drank on and stopped at a point to eulogize the circus, but circumstances had overtaken him and everyone was too drunk to listen.

Only Madame López noticed Mick's eyes fixated on Trina. For a while now he'd been in love with her and her trips on motorbikes with boys intensified this love. She'd fallen by the wayside, picked herself up, her re-emergence like the coming together of many bits of glass. Her smile broke now like a spray of blossoms. Her teeth sparkled, her lips orange from lipstick and radiating. Madame López's eyes became quizzical. She purred like a cat. Mick had been so lonely all his life, travelling in England and Ireland. There'd been the odd affair, more extravagant courtships than affairs, now in old age he longed for it, young flesh and Trina seemed suitably fallen, riding off with young men, sitting by the sea with them, her laughter gushing and her eyes dancing. Broken, in mental hospitals, he'd preferred her, her entrenchment, her doll-like reserve. Maybe it was something in all of them, a liking for disaster. Now at ease he resented Trina, wanted to abuse her lasciviously. But were her eyes on Tim? Tim's Russian claim he resented; yet something deeply Eastern often showed in Tim, an intensity, an arrested tremor, a sense of shock. Though dark his eyebrows were rubbed by blond and in spite of Mick's criticism they shone. He was a male mystic, a country man dominated by wild and tugging thoughts. His moment of conception had been when a Russian boat docked in Galway, his unease was inspired by this, he was a young man of no continent.

You could see them in Madame López's eyes again, the straggling poppies of Andalusia, the forewarnings of war, speckles of black on the red, guns in the corn fields, guns in the gipsy caravans.

If there were poppies in Madame López's eyes there were marigolds in Tim's, not the marigolds of war in Jan's eyes but the marigolds of Russia, eastern golds and browns. Marigolds were the flowers of autumn. They were also the flowers of a young man's flesh. Trina's eyes were lighter now and as they all began drinking again the caravan swayed, the lion growled, the crocodile barked. It was getting late. Madame López had her arm about Mick. Trina had her arm about Tim. Jan spoke to his glass of wine. He repeated them, over and over again, his wife's wrong doings. The Protestant church chimed two.

'I brought entertainment to a land now that hasn't even given me a pension,' Mick grumbled, 'I brought joy to a land embittered by its own poisoned hearts and what do I get back?'

He saw her eyes, gleaming. He wanted to reach to her and suggest at worst tenderness but she didn't seem to notice his plea. She slept with many young men he was sure; he resented her for it, not bearing the banners of his own puritan morality but even if she did he wanted to benefit from it. He wanted to spend the last night of the circus in the arms of a young woman. He recalled it again, sex, devouring scents of pubic hair, the startled nipples and the legs risen into the air. He wanted again to feel a body next to his, not a lion's or a crocodile's but a woman's. And Trina

103

could be called a woman now having relinquished madness and becoming gay and joyous.

But Tim was in his way. She had her eye on Tim. Tim didn't force her arms off him and her smile was bathed by dim light. Mick became angry.

He remembered his mother saying he'd come to no good and thought how right she was. He remembered his trail of solicitor brothers. He remembered the big house and his rejection by Ireland. He remembered youth and his wild fling and felt it was all worth it.

'I have two foolish daughters,' Madame López said, 'Money grabbers. They make chips all the time. I tell them, go to Spain, see Granada, see Sevilla. They stare. Fish and chips is right, cold fish. Ha. Ha.' She laughed, inspired by gloating. Jan said love is the worst thing in the world, the Russians the second worst. Trina's arm was about Tim. Tim sang a song in Irish. 'Cad a dhéanfaimíd Feasta gan Adhmad?' 'What shall We do Anymore Without Wood?' It was a song about the felling of wood in Stuart Ireland, time the British came and cut down the flourishing forests, time the Gaelic lords went and the pheasants went silent and the native entertainers, the harpers, the bards, only to flee for centuries through hedge and lake, imparting a poem by Virgil or a verse by Ovid to those starved for their native culture. The song could not have been more timely for Mick interpreted it for the others and he saw them, the circus people, as bearing on a great tradition, the subterfuge of entertainment.

He remembered the times they'd journeyed through Ireland when there'd been no television, the small towns in Kerry, the birds assembling for autumn, winter coming, the gales sweeping in but they going on, the bugles, the lions, the snatches from Shakespeare, the notes from *Il Trovatore*. He remembered a string of things, the venues, the small sacrifices made to see him, the nuns, the priests the maids, the affluent and the deprived combing for a vision of him.

104

Now all was changed, but if it was changed there was the solicitude of song, Tim's song, which put everything in its proper order, heroism, sacrifice, faith. He'd gone on against a mine of disabilities.

Madame López read his eyes and composed a speech from these things. Hers was the eulogy. They'd brought joy, pain, grief, laughter and now with their absence she compared their lot to a turning point in Irish history, the birds going from the trees, the trees going from Ireland and a silence coming, a parching silence that had lasted hundreds of years. They had at least brought a note of music to the silence.

Jan's eyes were the first to glow with tears. Maybe he was crying about his wife, not the circus. But Tim's face suddenly strengthened, the hollows of a young man's face and he said, 'Things that are beautiful never die.' His whole life, maybe, he'd seek to implement that theory, straining against obstacles. But now his faith inspired them all and the tears came, the last bottles drained and music came from nowhere, a fiddle, a tin whistle as senses drowsed and no one looked at one another.

Later, much later, thoughts of carnality washed from him like sin, Mick walked towards Trina's caravan, expecting to see her sleeping with Tim. But what surprised him was the fact that before he reached the caravan he heard a song, this time not in Irish but in Russian, verifying Tim's claim to be Russian.

Inside Tim was not sleeping with Trina but singing her to sleep. All Mick's thoughts of seduction vanished for ever as he realized that perhaps Trina wasn't such a wilful one as he thought but vulnerable too like him and that Tim, far from having carnal designs on her, had helped her, little by little, in the mental hospitals of Ireland, as she broke down crying, bringing her flowers, comforting her. The world still had a place for innocence. With that Mick left the enclosure outside Trina's caravan and made off to bed. A few more stars had struggled through. The caravans lay silent, the lights one by one going out. The Protestant church bell chimed as Mick opened the door of his caravan, looking around for the last time on the gaiety and the dereliction. He slept quietly, the mad race of circus Ireland careering over his mind, the jugglers, the dancers, the singers as a song like Madame López's rose in him, blocking out everything except the memory of the sea sparkling in early summer as caravans headed West.

Protestant Boy

It was not an edifying place to meet anyone but now, writing from a London bedsitter, curiously right, curiously Irish, totally unforgettable. Butlin's Holiday Camp, County Meath, a fortress by the ocean, sand running alongside it and for the imaginative thoughts of a reeling ocean, the one that divided Ireland from England.

One couldn't call it a sea. One has to exaggerate because it had all the qualities of an ocean, sand in the storm, sand in the hair, huge waves that shot up like explosions, dying again, leaving one to walks by the railway tracks, along the shore.

He was thirteen when I met him. There with an acrimonious Belfast aunt. What a horrible place Belfast must be I felt from her, her eyes like a lazy snake's and her teeth long gone and little bereaved. She held his hand and looked at me, from Galway, as though I was a sinner.

Yet friendship struck up – Danny was his name; a stout Protestant name Daniel, the thunder of Presbyterian choruses in it, but Danny was more. In a nation that knew or understood little of love Danny had rapturous smiles, a love of song, a voluminous stamp collection according to himself and a passion for the world of books.

I knew by his accent he was not like his aunt; she had an accent like old and mouldy saucers breaking. He spoke half like Queen Elizabeth's children, a bit like the children in 'Lassie' films. He was out of the ordinary. That was for sure.

I wandered Butlin's Holiday Camp with him, climbed

amusements with him, ate shoals of candyfloss, wandered in and out of a plethora of contests, contests for beautiful children, beautiful grannies, buoyant mums, dotty babies.

And then there was always the Irish Sea pounding away. If you wanted to escape the indignity of the modern world all you had to do was wander beaches Cuehullain had once trod on his way to the North country.

I wrote to him once or twice. My heart had danced at our relationship. I felt, hoped for many prospects. But I lived in a tight family set-up in Galway and couldn't visit him despite many invitations. He lived with his father outside Belfast; a big house. I was given to believe his father was wealthy. His mother was long dead and thereby he was hauled around by a variety of maiden aunts lower on the social scale than his father.

He wrote to me more than I wrote to him, long letters about the school he attended on the North Antrim coast, the ocean wailing, crashing on cliffs. He studied with the Protestant elite of Ulster. But I didn't see him as any different from me despite the fact that at Butlin's Holiday Camp, County Meath, I'd gone to a Catholic church and he to a Presbyterian one.

Letters stopped when I was about fifteen or sixteen, the first urgency of adolescence over and I slipping into a trough of non-communication, non-alignment with anyone. Danny was sent to the back of my mind; he did not reappear until some years later when I had entered the halls of University College, Dublin. I met him at a Student Christian Movement meeting, a ball of dazzling black hair, a jersey ripe as the tomatoes that grew in his father's green-houses. At first I couldn't place him as he approached me but the memory of his smile did not elude me and the eyes that were heightened, brown on a wet football.

'Hello, I'm Danny McNulty. Do you remember me?' he said. He was studying at Queen's University, Belfast, a degree in French literature. I was studying the old dunces of

Anglo-Irish literature. I smiled. Years it had been, but here was a certainty; Danny had something, simplicity maybe. Topics were discussed at the meeting, South Africa, Brazil, Northern Ireland. Since my last having seen Danny the North of Ireland had blossomed into a bed of violence, all shapes, nuances of violence, a cruelty there akin to Gestapo Germany, people maiming, murdering, mutilating and yet students still spoke of it as a cause.

The Provisional I.R.A. who had just begun their bombing campaign were right. At least they challenged the inertia of this empire of stuffy landowners and villainous, tweed coat sporting, pipe-smoking factory owners.

Danny had come with some Belfast friends, but alone we retired to a tobacco coloured pub where we spoke about the years, schooldays, now, politics. He'd abandoned home he said one minute, renounced his father; next minute he invited me to his father's home. I didn't get there for three years; not until I had nearly finished at college.

It was May. We'd contacted one another on and off. Now it came to reality, a visit to Danny's home. The sun blazed. An avenue led to a house packed away in the fields, a slate grey house with windows like devouring eyes.

I walked up the avenue, rucksack on my back. I'd hitched from Dublin, crossing the border near Dundalk. The clouds now were pasted in the sky like daisies. Danny was standing at the door. His hair had grown longer, his shirt now was saffron. His smile hadn't changed.

I knew I was in the heart of Protestant Ulster but I understood no fear, a sense of glee. This house with its chinks of stained glass, its prehistoric plants, its maid like a stalworthy druid, all conformed exactly with my idea of what Protestant Ulster should be. We were surrounded by cossetted Presbyterian churches, a defiant puritanism, and evidence everywhere of toil and discipline, discipline inner as well as outer. After all these people were so provoked by the republicans, weren't they, by a legion of imaginary devils all carrying shillelaghs and by the gunmen, merciless in their claim on life. Often a country policeman was called to death by them. Sometimes a farmer, his wife, his child.

Mercy was gratuitous in Ulster. It fell usually by coincidence rather than by design. There were the Protestant para-militaries too but their death toll wasn't known here; the weight of their justice belonged elsewhere.

Danny's father looked more like the gardener than a stalworth Unionist. He was gentle. The table was spread, brown bread, cold chicken, potato and cucumber salad. An Edwardian lady eyed us uneasily from the wall. I spoke about my examinations. Danny remarked on the sporadic relationship we'd had. He mentioned in passing that the aunt with whom he'd first met me had been killed by a bomb in Belfast. His father spoke of golf, the ocean, the year's tomatoes, Dublin, Buswells Hotel, the places there that most accommodated his northern sense of propriety and comfort. 'They tell me that Dublin's disappearing,' he said, 'I hope to visit it one of these days to catch up on its trail.'

Danny's room bore a picture of a guru, a bushel of lupins beneath the apparition. He'd been hooked by a band of eastern mystics in Belfast who occasionally wore white alongside grocery shops where shop-keepers were shot dead. Danny had become mystic, pacifist, obedient to inner laws in a province of violent conflagration. I had but three days there talking, taking strolls, devouring brown bread, visiting cottages, all abundant with photographs of Her Majesty the Queen with an occasional place for His Royal Highness Prince Philip. People were curious, friendly with me. Was I or wasn't I in the I.R.A.?

College over, I lived in Dublin for two years with a girl, working as a social worker by a kind of mistake, people thinking an English degree qualified me to work with young offenders in Dublin's poverty wrenched city centre.

The news that Danny or at least someone with his name and address had been convicted in Belfast of possession of

110

arms was odd to me, odder that he was a member of the
Provisional I.R.A. He got off lightly, six months in jail. His
background I suppose neutralized the odium of his crime.

I went to Belfast on a tour of community centres on the
Catholic-Protestant borderline and discovered the real heroes, these community workers who crossed the Catholic and
Protestant dividing lines. It occurred to me to try to contact
Danny. I didn't know where I'd begin. He'd surely be
thrown out of home. So I went back to Dublin and met him
in an American hamburger joint late one spring night when
the cashier was wearing a snowdrop.

He was wearing a leather jacket, was with a woman, her
hair henna. She was German. He'd joined the Provos, he
said, because his people had unjustly conquered the northern
province of Ireland. He was fighting people like his father
who bind the working class to servitude. The back-streets of
Belfast were an agony he said. Once the people rise one
must choose where to throw your lot. He'd chosen the army
of the militant Catholics.

He looked like a gay revolutionary, a woman by his side.
He said nothing of what he was doing now or where he was
going. Libya maybe. Amsterdam?

I remembered one thing he'd said to me in Butlin's years
before as a child; it came like a very lucid flash of lightning.
He'd said, a child in a tee-shirt on a beach: 'The Irish are
soldiers, aren't they? Irishmen always fight. Will we fight
too?'

I thought him a madman on the loose and would
somehow have told him he was acting from class guilt, that
the I.R.A. were no heroes, they were as separate from the
Irish people as the brine from the Atlantic ocean, an echo of
an old disease, Republicanism. I knew the faces of the poor
deprived of Dublin. Would Patrick Pearse ever have saved
them?

Anyway, like it or not, I was becoming bitter in myself.
My relationship with my girlfriend was breaking up.

111

Dublin, despite American hamburger joints and garish boutiques, was as it traditionally had been, full of sores, and one December morning, face to coast of Wales, I left, an emigrant in a leather jacket. I had a job in London, in the East End, having been appropriately interviewed.

I was without my woman. I was free. That curdling town was left behind, Dublin, unique for its barbed wit and its vengeful stares. I loved something of it though, the hallowed flight of a gull, the trustful silence of models in Grafton Street windows, a coffee shop, a tree, a church which brought rich and poor together down an alley-way.

But it wasn't Dublin that haunted so much in London. It was Danny. The bits and pieces of his life, so strange, our meetings, each like a card in a Tarot reading. The night I'd met him in Dublin I'd given him my address and after five months in London something that I interpreted as a miracle happened. A letter came, forwarded from my former Dublin flat, from Danny. He had heard I'd gone to live in London. He was on his way there himself, leaving Belfast and its plethora of gospel halls.

I met him in Camden Town one evening, in a quiet pub. He'd left the Provos, witnessed the brutality of a girl being tarred and feathered, suffered the knowledge that a boy who'd been his friend had been shot dead in the head on the pretext of being an informer. The howling wind of Irish patriotism had come home to him. It had been fun for a while, guns, halls in Belfast, another race, the Northern Catholic race.

His father had kicked him out of home originally not for being a member of the I.R.A. but for bringing a Catholic girl home and sleeping with her in the house.

I had been O.K. My visit. At least he hadn't slept with me.

He'd got to know much of the Catholic underground of Belfast, the I.R.A. training centres, the prayers, the aspirations, the underground newspapers, the violent cause linked into the aura of rosary beads. He'd fought once or twice, fought out of a sense that here were a people robbed of life by people like his father, that the goods in Northern Ireland had been handed up to a steadfast hard-working Protestant deity, that there was a killing weight on Catholic shoulders. But perhaps it was more than a few acts of violence that halted his progress as a violent revolutionary. It was a kind of encounter with the real nature of his involvement in life, flirtation. The Protestant boy left Belfast, appalled by violence, appalled by his own part in it, returning somehow to the sanctity of his feelings, feelings that were around when I visited his home and found a picture of an Indian guru there.

Danny got a job as a supply teacher in a very liberal school. I worked with hard cases and he visited me once or twice as I did drama classes with young people society had jilted. It was fun. A humour arose from those young people and for the first time a real relationship began between me and Danny. Two young Irishmen, albeit from different parts of Ireland, we spent a lot of time together. I didn't see much of women now, wounded in Ireland, and Danny somehow looked younger. We saw films, plays together, perhaps that old bird the phoenix shaping in our lives.

I knew there were some things Danny didn't tell me and I really didn't want to know the circumstances of his joining the I.R.A., the inverted loyalism; once circumcised by devilish nationalism you can't get away from it. Maybe it was a look that began on his face, a haunting, a fear, nightmares when he stayed with me. I realized now he'd walked into the I.R.A. not out of conviction but as he'd stumbled into many things, Butlin's, the Student Christian Movement, eastern religion. It had been a cause like a deflated tricolour. It had been a protest against a part of himself, the hard-working steadfast Protestant part.

I don't take sides, but one thing I know now, that violence is a disease, that once touched by its madness you cannot

113

escape it call it what you will, Marxism, Loyalism, Nationalism. Danny had ventured too far, the skeleton of an idea lingering in him, that of man's evil to man.

We went to Cambridge one day in April. There were blue-bells everywhere, the occasional shower. Danny spoke of how he had begun to understand his own people again, the North of Ireland Protestants; they weren't oppressors. Like the whites in America they were there. They asked only to be left alone. I found this difficult to take but he elaborated; the Protestants of Northern Ireland were a law unto themselves. They had always, always been painted as lunatics. Until people tried to understand something of their inevitable integrity there would never be peace in Ireland.

Some few weeks later Danny was dead. He'd fallen under a train. At Paddington. That's how the story went.

But I knew he'd been pushed by a para-military, by the ghost of the old croney Mother Ireland, I don't know, by an idea; once you dabble in black magic you cannot leave it, once you stir the waters of death you can't get away from the notion of death, the death of conscience, the death of decision, the death of common sense.

I went to see a film about Northern Ireland some weeks after Danny died. It showed how the Republicans were the good guys, fighting a war of liberation. There were plenty of young English people around, punk ladies, women in chiffon scarves, the gay elite of England, young men from the Gay Liberation Movement.

I listened to a speech afterwards about the Republican movement and its fight against British imperialism and its Loyalist supporters in Ireland. I thought of Danny, of Danny's people, the Protestants of Ulster, once freedom fighters, now convicted by history.

I imagined the little cottages in Antrim, the air of enterprise, the mountain breezes blowing pages of a draconian Bible open. I walked out. I knew I could never again return to an ideology that made criminals of an entire race. I

114

walked through the streets of London. News on the hoardings was of more bombings. I wondered if I'd ever lose her, that lady Mother Ireland, who created a pageant out of death and atrocity, but I knew that at least something had triumphed, one note on a bagpipe in a Glen in Antrim. At least somewhere inside myself I knew that they existed, Danny's people, they weren't a figment of anyone's political imagination. They were real.

Teddyboys

With a curious sultry look they waited, diamonds in their eyes, and handkerchiefs, thick and scarlet, in their pockets. They stood around, lying against the bank corner, shouldering some extraordinary responsibility, keeping imagination, growth, hope alive in a small Irish town some time around the beginning of the sixties.

Then mysteriously they disappeared; all but one, Jamesy Clarke, gone to Birmingham, London, leaving one solitary teddyboy to hoist his red carnation. It was a lovely spring when they left. I was sorry they'd gone. But there was Jamesy.

He bit his lip with a kind of sullen spite. His eyes glinted, topaz. His hair gleamed. His shirts were scarlet and his tie blue with white polka dots.

As spring came early young men dived into the weir.

I wanted, against this background of river teeming with salmon, to congratulate Jamesy Clarke for staying to keep the spirit of dashing dress and sultry eyes alive. Instead I followed him, ever curious, watching each step he took knowing him to be unusually beautiful and somewhat beloved by the Gods. Though nine years of age, going on ten, I knew about these Gods. An old fisherman by the Suck had once said, 'The Gods always protect those who are doomed.' I harboured this information. I told no one.

Jamesy had stayed to look after his widowed mother. He lived in the 'Terrace' with her, behind a huge sign for Guinness, bottles abandoned, usually broken, children running about, a cry and a whine rising from them that aggravated the nerves and haunted like other signs of poverty haunted, dolls broken and destroyed, old men leaning against the men's lavatory, drunken and abused. His mother was allegedly dying from an unspoken disease, sitting among statues of Mary, that surrounded her like meringues, and cough-bottle smelling irises.

I'd never actually seen his mother. But I knew she dominated the tone of Jamesy's life, the prayers, the supplications, the calling on Our Lady of Fatima. Our Lady of Fatima was very popular in our town. She adorned most houses, in some more agonized than others, and a remarkable statement under her in my aunt's house: 'Eventually my pure heart will prevail.'

The fields about the river were radiant with buttercups, fluff amassed and fled over the Green and the odd youngster swam. I noticed Jamesy swimming a few times, always by himself, always when evening came, taking off his clothes, laying them in the stillness, jumping into the water in scarlet trunks. He never saw me. He wasn't supposed to. Like a little emissary of the Gods I wandered about, taking note, keeping check, always acute and waiting for any circumstance which could do him harm. He was much too precious to me. His shirts, scarlet and blue, impressed me more than Walt Disney movies. But it was his eyes that awed me more than anything, eyes faraway as the Connemara mountains and yet near, near in sympathy and in sensation, eyes that saw and kept their distance.

Scandal broke like mouldy Guinness when apparently Jamesy was caught in the launderette making love to a girl. The girl was whizzed off to England. Clouds of June gathered; the Elizabethan fortress by the river stood out, one of the last outposts of the Queen in Connaught. Jamesy kept his distance. He didn't seem troubled or disturbed by scandal. He went his way. It was as though this girl was like washing on the line. She hadn't altered his life, hadn't changed him.

He smoked cigarettes by the bank corner, alone there now. Their scents accumulated in my nostrils. I took to naming cigarettes like one would flowers. A mantra rose in my mind that ordered and preoccupied a summer: Gypsy Annie, Sailor Tim. I called cigarette brands new names. I exploited all the knowledge I had of the perverse and applied it to Jamesy's cigarettes.

Ancient women sold pike in the Square. Sometimes they looked to the sky. They'd never seen a summer like this, broken cloud, imminent heat.

Old men wiped their foreheads and engrossed people in conversation about the Black and Tans. Everything harkened back; to the Rising, to the War of Independence, to the Civil War. Forgotten heroes and cowards were discussed and debated. The mental hospital looked particularly threatening; as though at any moment it was going to lurch out and grab. Jamesy swam. He had no part in conversation about the rising, in talk of new jobs or new factories. Where he was financed from I don't know but he led a beautiful life and if it hadn't been for him the summer would not have been exciting and I would not have eagerly waited for the holidays when I could follow him along the railway tracks, always at a distance, until he came to a different part of the river from the one he swam in, sitting there, thinking.

When he started going out with a tailor's daughter I was horrified. I knew by the way she dressed she did not have his sense of colour. She walked with an absence of dignity. His arm always hung on her shoulder in a half-hearted way and she led him away from the familiar spots, the bank corner, the river.

I saw them go to a film. I observed him desert the summer twilights. I felt like writing to his friends in England, asking them to come back and send him out or feeding his mother with poison to make her complaint worse. Even the hold his

118

mother's disease had on him seemed negligible in comparison to this girl's.

I noticed the actresses who starred in the film they went to see, Audrey Hepburn, Lana Turner, and privately held them responsible. I looked up at Lana Turner one night when they'd entered the cinema and told her I would put a curse on her.

I learnt about curses from a mad stocky aunt who lived in the country, was once regarded with affection by all our family until an uncle had a mongoloid child. Then attention diverted from her and she started cursing everyone, making dolls of them and putting them in fields of corn. I knew it worked. About the time she did one of my mother, my mother went to hospital. I knew it was an awful thing to do. But there was too much at stake.

The more I cursed her though, the more defiant Lana Turner looked, her breasts seemed almost barer. I stopped cursing her and started swearing at her, swearing at her out loud. The local curate passed. He looked at me. I said, 'Hello Father.'

He wondered at a child staring at a poster of Lana Turner, calling her by all the foul names my father called my mother.

Come July young men basked by the river. The sun had broken through and an element of ecstasy had come to town, towels, bottles of orange thrown about. Ivy grew thick and dirty about the Elizabethan fortress, gnats made their home there and a royal humming commenced then, a humming and a distillation of the voices of gnats and flies.

The evenings were wild and crimson; clouds raged like different brands of lipstick. That's one thing I'll say for Jamesy Clarke, he still took the odd swim by himself. In the silence after twilight he took off his clothes and dived into the water. Threads were whispered over the grass by the spiders. Wet descended. The splash of water reverberated. There were moments of silence when he just urged through

119

the water. I waited across the field, my head in my lap. If I could I would have built him a golden bridge out of here. I knew all that was piled against him, class, the time that was in it, his mother. It no longer mattered to me that this town should have him. What I wanted for him was a future in which he could puff on smart cigarettes in idyllic circumstances. But much as I racked my brain I could think of nowhere to place him. London and Birmingham sounded too dour, Fatima was already peopled by statues of the Blessed Virgin and other places I knew of I was uncertain of, Paris, Rome. There just might have been a place for him in Hollywood but I knew him to be too elegant for it, there were more than likely simpler and more beautiful places in the United States into which he could have fitted. I wanted him more than anything to be safe, though safe from what I didn't know.

He held his girlfriend's hand about town. He sat on the fair Green with her. He hugged her to him. He'd discarded jackets and wore orange tee-shirts. A bracelet banded his arm, narrowly scathing hairs on his skin which was the colour of hot honey. I looked to the sky above them, clouds like rockets in it. Perhaps his girlfriend did have something after all, a hunch of his existence. Nobody could have seduced him for so much time away from bank corner or river without responding to something in him. I forgave her. I gave up ownership. I played with the notion of being present at their marriage. I had it already arranged in my mind. He'd be dressed in white. She in blue. There'd be marigolds as there were outside the courthouse and his mother, virtually dead, would be in a moveable bed in the church.

Then one day things changed. The weather broke. Clouds which had been threatening, sending shadows coursing over wheat and water, now plunged into rain. The heat evaporated and a sudden cold absorbed all that was beautiful, warmth in old stone, the preening of daisies in side-walk crevices. I shook inside. I had to stay in. I played with dinkies. I looked through books. I found no information relevant to life. I burnt a total of three books one evening, two about horses and one an adventure story set in Surrey. I became like a little censor, impatient and ravaging anything that didn't immediately allow one in on the mystery of being. Dickens was merely sent back to the library. He was lucky.

I wrote a letter to Jamesy; he stood stranded by rain.

Dear Jamesy,
I hate the rain. I wish I lived in a country where it didn't rain. How are you? I'm not too well.
I've decided I don't like books anymore. I prefer things like clothes. My mother keeps giving out; she was giving out when the sun was shining and she gives out when it's raining. How's your mother? I said a prayer to Our Lady of Fatima for her yesterday.
It's raining outside now, I'm going to draw a picture of Mecca. I was just reading about Mecca where all the Moslems go. I'm going to draw a picture of it and colour it in. See you soon I hope.

Desmond.

I didn't send the letter of course. I coloured it in too, drawing pictures of teddyboys along the sides. I also drew a scarlet heart, pierced by an arrow, the number three, emphasising it in blue, and a tree trunk.

I bore it with me for a while until one day it fell out of my pocket, the colours washing into the rain.

Jamesy had had a row with his girlfriend. That was obvious when the sun shone again. He looked disgruntled. An old woman, member of a myriad confraternities, reported that he spat on the pavement on front of her. 'Disgusting,' the lady said. 'Disgusting,' my mother agreed. 'A cur,' the lady said. 'A cur,' my mother said. And the lady added,

'What do you expect from the likes of him. His eyes,' she screeched with outrage, 'his beady eyes.'

It was true. Jamesy's eyes had changed, become pained, narrow, fallen from grace. He wore a white jacket, always clean though in his despair, and his features knotted in disgruntlement as cold winds blew and a flotsam of old ladies wandered the town, gossiping, discussing all shapes of misdemeanour with one another in highly-pitched, off-centre voices.

Jamesy edged into the voice of autumn, his dislocation, his pain, and his eyes spitting, a venom in them now.

He began seeing his girlfriend again. This time he tugged her about town. She was a vehicle he pushed and swayed. Though a tailor's daughter she had her good points, grace I had to admit, and an almond colour in her hair, always combed and arranged to a kind of exactitude.

Lana Turner never graced our cinema again. There were posters which showed motor-bicycles or men in leather jackets, their faces screwed up as they unleashed a punch on someone. I lost Jamesy on his trail more than often.

Women whispered about Our Lady of Fatima now as though she was threatening them. Voices spoke of death, a faint shell-shocked murmuring each time a member of the community passed away. Death was wed into our town like a sister, a nucleus about which to whisper, a kind of alley-way to the Divine.

Almost as suddenly as it went, the fine weather returned, revealing a curious harvest, tractors in the fields, farmers, brown as river slime, on bicycles. Then young men of town returned to the river. They were quieter now, something was pulling out of their lives, summer, imperceptibly, like a tide.

Northern Protestants had come and gone, daubing a poster on the mill overlooking the weir, 'What shall it profit a man; if he shall gain the whole world, and lose his own soul?'

I couldn't find Jamesy. There was no sign of him in the evenings, swimming. I started an odyssey, seeking him through field and wood. Birds called. I thought I heard Indians once or twice. Horses lazed about, the last flowers of summer sung with bees, standing above the grass, lime and gold. The bold lettering of the poster above the weir was in my mind, its message was absent. I did not understand it.

My travels led me to wood and to Georgian house lying outside the town. I hadn't forgotten Jamesy but I kept looking, pretending to myself I'd see him in far-flung places.

I sat on a hill one day and looked at the river beyond. My tee-shirt was red. My mind was tranquil. I used the moment to think of Jamesy, his eyes, his anguish. I had seen that anguish cutting into his face in the course of the summer, into his eyes, his cheekbones, his mouth. I had seen a sculpture gradually realizing itself and the sculpture, like beautiful stamps, like stained glass in the church, spoke of an element of human nature I did not understand but knew was there, grief. It was manifest in Jamesy. I wondered about his mother, her journey towards death, his attitude to it, his solitary trails about town, the manifold cigarettes, the grimaces.

I imagined his mother's bedroom as I had visualized it many times, one statue standing out among the statues of Mary, that of Our Lady of Fatima, notable for her beauty and the snake writhing at her feet. That snake I identified now as a curse, the one that blighted Jamesy's face, the one that blighted Ireland, trodden on by the benign feet of one whose purity might as she claimed ultimately prevail.

My searching for Jamesy was becoming more spurious, a kind of game now, an unspoken fantasy; gone was the grandeur of odyssey. I observed thicket, nettle and flower.

Then one evening late in August unexpectedly I came on Jamesy. It was virtually dark, by the river, letters standing out on the poster, and as I wandered by the Elizabethan fortress noise became apparent to me. I looked over a hedge. There in the grass by a tributary of the river Jamesy was making love to the tailor's daughter.

123

The skirmish of a bird with a bush could not have been more noiseless than me, the running of an otter in the grass. I made my way home, shaken by what I had seen.

I hated him, yet I hated him with a hatred that transcended Jamesy. I hated him for what he was doing, for the image he had given me, for this new distortion on stained glass.

I wanted to share his simplicity, an empathy with his face. But there was more to him than a face and in the silence of my room, a wind rushing on the river outside as swans flew over, in the tradition of my rural aunt, in the tradition of gypsies and country Irish people rummaging with broken dolls, I cursed Jamesy.

He should not have told me what I didn't want to know, that the human spirit is tarnished.

Jamesy's girlfriend left town, a silent pageant by the station, she was going to a job in Dublin. He was there to say goodbye to her, a teddyboy on a summer day, platform shorn of all but marigolds. I watched him now, assisting him towards his doom.

He swam again in summer evenings alone, silently racing across dew moistened grass to dive into the water and one evening when I wasn't looking he was drowned.

I wanted to tell everyone it was me who did it, I wanted to announce my guilt and be penalized for it. But in my tee-shirt red as a balloon in the late summer radiance no one listened; I was denied any sense of retribution. I was ignored.

His funeral occurred two days before I returned to school. Young girls with the look of girls from the 'Terrace', faces pinched and yet knowledgeable, marched behind a hearse piled with masses of red carnations. He had many cousins, young females, and thereby many wreaths were donated.

The town came out in throngs, people loving funerals, and he being young, they accepted his death, excusing him all, his background, his spitting on the cement as he passed old ladies.

'Sure he stayed to look after his mother,' women slurred, and his mother, risen from her deathbed, looking fine and healthy, was there, a woman in black with a scarf of emerald and white on her head.

The prayers were read; a woman of the community, respectable, stood out from the crowd, a single tear in her eye.

Glass was reflected around the cemetery, domes bearing images of the sky and other wreaths and when they were all gone I stayed.

I knew he had departed for ever, his death seemed inevitable like so many things, autumn, and the poster on the weir.

I told him I was sorry. I apologised. I knew, however, the grief of his death would fill my life and whether I was responsible or not I'd always see him wherever I went, his eyes, his tie with the colonnade of polka dots.

His mother assumed perfect health in the next few months, whether assisted by Our Lady of Fatima or not I'll never know, but one thing I understood, over school books, in the anguish of the classroom I knew by looking out the window that somehow she had triumphed as she said she would. The lady with iron eyes, blue drapes on her robe, her hands joined in prayer and her feet squelching a snake, had prevailed.

Our Lady of Fatima, touchstone of the miraculous, had claimed unto herself a soul before it knew the damp of winter or the drought that issued from the human heart.

Southern Birds

Come this time of year there were huge aggravated cloud patterns in the sky and a place, usually just forlorn, took on a harsh elemental quality as though it had not been built by modern estate planners but by prehistoric forces. The tinkers camped nearby; boys lounged in the cemetery, smoking dope, drinking sherry. At night a whine often rose from the youth club where a record played for a while, couples jived hesitantly; then for lack of interest silence coming. The action took place at the cemetery, the young people of Ballyfermot integrating, getting drunk or stoned silly.

Dublin is a beautiful city, a Viking city. There are inspiring inlets, but Ballyfermot is a devil's dream. Just before you come to the Midlands it lies, another city altogether, an embarrassment, a cage.

Jeremy grew up in Ballyfermot; he was a child of this metropolis, a youth in blue denim. In Ballyfermot he had acquired a certain fame, having written a play about a pie-bald horse that toured community centres. His friend Leo had played the horse. Altogether there was comradeship between them, a fatalistic one, friends against the presaging sky, two boys just out of school.

Schools in Ballyfermot held many statues, statues of Mary, statues of Joseph, a zoo of statues, ones with chipped noses and varnished nails.

Their parents sometimes looked like statues. When they went with the 'bad' boys, the graveside boys, those who

126

consumed sherry, smoked dope, became daft as deformed trees under the influence of alcohol and drugs.

Sometimes one detected an anti-British slogan, visiting relatives from the North daubing their trade mark 'Brits Out' on the garden walls; but the North was miles from here; there were different problems, little bread and what there was of bread stale and unwholesome. This was the product of a poets' revolution, the Bible of Irish politicians, the 1916 revolution.

A grim, dirty, seedy, unwanted estate, it spread, enlarging and with it growing a culture, the culture in Jeremy's and Leo's heads, the culture of search. For all the young people here searched, whether through drugs or drink, they sought ways out. Some took them on a boat. One or two boys had gone North and joined the Provos but they were few and usually came of wildly Republican backgrounds.

Jeremy however wrote plays and if he did go with the others it was really as an outsider.

Physically he was tall and it was his face one noticed most, full of changes of expression, a fullness and a kindness, a leniency that more than often got him into trouble. He was 'soft' his mother cried, vulnerable and attractive to women. Nuns had a special liking for him, the black and grey nuns of Ballyfermot. Unlike the other boys he was shy, polite and, if he didn't dress too neatly, he had a manner that one earnestly trusted.

Leo, smaller than him, had trusted his friend for a long time. They'd gone to vocational school together and now finished, harboured joints over Ballyfermot, pausing, looking down on a city they knew not to have been made of pearls and diamonds but composed of seedy night clubs, mannequins escaped from colour advertisements, run down pubs and modern buildings, billowing like blankets on a line.

'Let's go somewhere,' Leo suggested one night, the suggestion hardly reaching Jeremy's ear, he staring down, pondering on the faraway Liffey, lifting its skeleton finger against the night. Young men and women sat around, smoking, drinking. They heard trains passing, a sound that penetrated the moon.

Jeremy registered Leo's words at last. No job, no money; why not go away? But the eating problem of poverty prevailed. They required money to take leave of their environment. Leo got a job in a pub at night towards the end of August, he fiddled greatly, taking money from the till. Jeremy got a job in the convent, cleaning floors. It was arduous but Sister Mary Martha was full of stories about her childhood in Mayo, stories about banshees and headless horsemen, hovering over him like an overgrown leprechaun, she sprouting out of black shoes like a bad cabbage.

Some money early in September; indifferent to weather two youths, Jeremy eighteen, Leo nineteen, headed off towards Belfast, hitch-hiking past the airport.

Belfast they found to be a city of searing blackness; they stayed with Leo's aunt off the Falls Road. Rain splashed. Lights bloomed, naked, white, saracens rushed by in the deluge. Fish and chips were wrapped in Republican newspapers, prayers for dead soldiers, invocations of the many blessings of Our Lady Queen of Ireland for commandants who died in action and now filled the air of Milltown cemetery with their ghosts. Leo's aunt was quiet; she held back on discussion of years of tragedy. Resentment of the British army was everywhere, yet an odd fear of what would happen if they left. The Provos were never referred to by name but Jeremy understood their lordship.

There were gulls in Belfast, rain. But in his gut Jeremy hated it, this war torn city, boys just out of school in England standing around in uniform. There were words about King Billy and chiding remarks about the Pope. The young were endowed with the centuries as a gift, centuries of fear, of siege, of blind hatreds and winnowing Lagan breezes.

128

Jeremy saw them: paralysed, the young, Protestant and Catholic. He saw the British between them, teenagers, statues in the alley-ways. He wondered if anything would ever come between Catholics and Protestants other than British soldiers. He imagined delayed festivity, festivity coming for years, wondered what would speed it. Now there was silence, silence of streets, pattering rain, gutters gulping as street lamps reflected on the kind of black only Belfast knew.

They left Belfast, hitch-hiking around the coast, meeting a tinker in Ballymena who told them about the Ballinasloe horsefair and they turned in that direction, leaving the North of Ireland, a quarter of privation and uncertainty, heading South, towards the most ancient fair in Europe.

Ballyfermot sometimes crossed their minds but as it was autumn the strong whiff of leaves took their breath and senses away, leaves tidying themselves, little burdens of orange and gold outside rectories that looked as though they were about to blow away.

True to form the tinkers were there, hundreds of them, brightly painted caravans, all kinds of deceits painted. Madame Lucy reads the cups, Ziza Mandala sees your future in your palm. Smoke rose from caravans, always a little element of torture in it, the presence of autumn undefined but controlling things like smoke, bark with its odd mixture of scents.

The two boys wandered the town and got lodging in a house where Wolf Tone was reputed to have stayed once while visiting the fair. They slept in one big bed under a quilt that had all colours in it. It could indeed have been the end of the eighteenth century when Tone was rallying Catholics and Irish Protestants to revolution.

Leo was smaller than Jeremy and as ducks wandered farms outside Ballinasloe they lay close; realizing there was male kinship at least.

They'd spent little but now had fun drinking in the

129

amusement arcade, sharp shooting. Ballinasloe exploded, dynamite of stars and big wheel.

They met Catriona in a pub, black haired woman sitting over a pint of Guinness as though it imposed a threat. How conversation between them began they couldn't remember afterwards, except that she kept smattering cigarette ashes on the floor and Jeremy asked her about it, his mother referring to people who did this kind of thing as 'Low down Cork Street tripes.'

She philosophised about shaking ash on the floor, saying that the abandon of the gesture suited her personality. Her accent was Irish but she was quick to inform the boys that her mother had been an Irish tinker who had married into the English upper classes.

'We're here for the crack.' Leo told her, 'What are you here for?'

'I come because I'm one of the travelling people,' she said. 'Instinct. The instinct that heralds the Indian to the elk.'

No elk could be sighted in Ballinasloe, but Catriona was correct about the instinctive things; there were many gipsies with coal black Romany eyes, dogs that had strayed from Famine times, those tinker women with hair as of beaten copper and features that shot out like the bulbs of spring flowers.

Catriona had them buy her hot whiskey and then bought them Guinness. She lived in a caravan on the fair Green she said, having travelled from Kerry, drawn by horses.

She lived usually by the ocean, selling her paintings of mares to American or British tourists. She had come to Ballinasloe because she believed it was what the past demanded of her. The urgency with which she told them of her past was remarkable, the husband who'd drowned himself, her present solitude, her moments of creation, her life wedded now to the birds.

They returned to her caravan that evening. She gave them tea and whiskey and then courtesy let them take leave of her.

130

When they returned to the Green late the following day her caravan had gone and they in their inspiration decided to follow her.

Portumna, Nenagh, Limerick, Abbeyfeale; children cherished school satchels in small Irish towns. Outside Tralee they came to the village she spoke of and there they were directed towards her site.

A caravan, a dog they hadn't seen before, a cage outside the caravan with two Mongolian mice. Catriona came to the door. Behind her were mountains, rough and wild, and the ocean. She now looked like a rainbow of things, grief and abundant joy, abandon and mediocre uncertainty. She welcomed the boys; by now they were beginning to realize her mind had somewhat flown.

Nearby was a cottage which was her studio and after tea she led them there; it was a surprise, a revelation, horses of all kinds, mares like prehistoric mares, dots on white, tails like banners on them and manes like forked lightning. There were prizes she'd won around, trophies of one sort or another, certificates.

Catriona's accent moved between West of Ireland and upper-class English with a bit of Lancashire; her husband's accent. By the ocean she spoke of the legendary heroes of Ireland, the Tuatha de Danann. One wondered from her intensity if they would return. Night came over the sea, evening a ball rolled round and around.

They had tea again; Catriona spoke of life in an upper-class English home, tomatoes forever verging on ripeness, foetal green merging into red.

Her father was an aristocrat, wore green and purple jerseys. Her mother for that matter was an aristocrat too, Famine Irish, eyes that had gathered the horror of that time, horror of hunger. They'd loved one another but Catriona at sixteen had left the Benedictine nuns, a convent school, run away, taken up with gipsies who picked hops in Kent, married a Lancashireman, come to Ireland. Her dog's name

131

was O'Fogarthy, a proper name for a valiant mongrel who had the airs of a wolfhound.

They stayed in her studio; smell of paint in their dreams, Ballyfermot only in their nightmares, the cemetery, the river frozen with orange blooms. Songs of summer rose and merged into a Kerry autumn, birds gathered, disciplined regiments of them. The beady eyes of starlings stared at the imminent grey. They would take bag and baggage to azure places.

Jeremy wrote messages on the beach. Leo climbed mountains, encountered old men, men who stared at far-off peninsulas as though at the new world.

Rain came; the boys painted the house. They painted the caravans and performed little chores.

Although there were few trees around, tiny filaments of leaves arrived, haunting the light breezes.

Alone at night they laughed at Catriona, the stained glass window of her past. If it was true which probably it was it was also a fact she was a fine artist and Kerry and Limerick men who owned stores came and bought her wares, paintings of Irish horses dancing against the moon.

At night lying on separate mattresses they heard the banshee, a howling orchestrated sound. The wind was rushing through a gap in a stone wall, but to Jeremy it was the scream of a young soldier in Belfast, fragmented by an I.R.A. bullet, the wail of a siren over a Catholic domain, the hysteria of a thrush in some avenue in Belfast who witnesses a door-step killing. He got up, his body roused into an extravagent eroticism, walked into Catriona's caravan, lay by her and entered her, aware of a power in his body, the shedding of seed, the lonesomeness, the cry of sex.

She looked more like an Irish country girl after that. The following Saturday night both Jeremy and Leo got drunk in Tralee, cycled home on the same bicycle, both lying with her.

She was a strange woman, skin olive, a mixture of British

132

reserve and Irish coarseness. She was like a nun who wanted her body for herself but being generous gave herself. She wore raincoats in the early November rain, a farmer's wife now.

The Atlantic thundered in. Jeremy discerned saracen tanks in it.

Catriona drank whiskey with them in a nearby pub. She had returned to the first posture they'd noticed in her: distance. They made love to her but it was as though she was a passive thing, only giving, never demanding an iota, an echo of pleasure for herself.

It was Jeremy who first backed away, knowing he'd been liked by nuns. He stopped making love to her and Leo, somewhat touched by all the things that made up Jeremy, retreated too. They lived together again, the two boys, in the studio, and Catriona talked to the dog.

Her husband's body was washed in in Donegal, she said, on a May day more like autumn. They could never place an age on her; nor did they know if she told the truth, but she didn't give the impression of being a liar either; only a gifted artist.

She read the Ecclesiastes at night in a big King James Bible. They read comics or paperbacks. The dog read nothing. She talked about burying herself in the earth, as an artist should, merging with the clay, bringing forth a tree, a flower. She spoke of absolute abandon. She remarked on rainbows, on the southern flight of birds. If only her caravan could go straight south. She became less tinker, less gipsy, more young woman with purified features who was a painter, a seeker. She'd driven her husband mad, she said, too much of the creative within her. Creativity destroys, she said, the making, the healing of things. Man is made for the mundane. The inkling of beauty distracts and disturbs.

Whales peeled south. A procession of gulls went by, a seal visited the strand, an emissary from the sea. He returned. He would come back with the apocalypse.

133

.She was neither tinker or gipsy but painter. She was quite ordinary really and her very ordinariness distracted Jeremy and Leo; Leo spoke of the holiday being over. Jeremy thought of southern places, sand, sea that was blue.

The closeness of two companions, the absence of promiscuity changed Catriona, it refined her and her features emerged as an apparition, forehead, eyes, nose. She cooked for them. She read a Protestant Bible. Eventually she cracked up.

Her paintings were wild and uncontrollably joyous, but she, in her isolation, had developed the cancer of retribution; it was guilt, guilt over always leaving everything for the sake of articulated beauty, family, friends, husband. The hands that touch a canvas are the hands of a diseased person. The disease Jeremy decided is love of beauty.

A simple woman, she began speaking of nuns and birds; congregations of birds became gatherings of nuns. The bleat of birds heralded a Gregorian chant for her; English Catholicism, talk of redemption. She took to wearing short skirts, plastic coats that made her look like any young woman. She walked the beach. She gathered bark. Where was her madness perceptible? In her silence. In the strain of anguish on her face, eyes that became so blue they twisted an hallucination with them, the blue of a summer's day, southern blue.

Her husband had drowned himself. Why they didn't know. Only that if he hadn't something else would have happened to him. All they knew about him was he mended tin and always got the King of Hearts in cards despite his imminent death.

A priest visited one night, had tea, spoke about the Holy Father, told dirty jokes, informed them of a production by the amateur drama group in Tralee, eventually tried to convert them, was pushed into the night by Catriona. That night she seduced them both, gave something to them, anger, pain, took something from them, momentarily their

134

souls, souls made up of Ballyfermot nights, an endless longing for that which wasn't there.

They felt bereaved and shaken afterwards. In his nakedness Jeremy took a bottle of sour Guinness and began drinking it on the floor. Leo lay in bed with the woman. Jeremy wanted to destroy something in himself. He had been deceived by this woman. She had mutilated the order in him. Leo lived with the woman in the caravan while Jeremy made a house for himself in the studio. Winter was coming, anger, torment of wind and spray.

And then they knew she wanted them to go, their moment was over with her, her need for solitude again intact. She stopped speaking to them, made toast for herself, piled tinned peas on it. At gay moments in the night she conjured soup, but drank it herself.

The boys felt mouse-like, rejected, scared. The birds were gone.

They left Tralee one November morning, hitching to Dublin. Leo had slept with Catriona the previous night, but it was as though he'd picked up a woman in a dancehall and she'd got that kind of salacious pleasure from him. Jeremy's seed had leaked on a blanket that night. Nearby was the sea, angry remains of trees.

Catriona had been up painting when they left. She said goodbye, but her heart wasn't in the farewell; they were tourists who'd come and were going now.

Back in Dublin they found the city had shrunken, all the jobs grabbed up; Grafton Street was thronged with record sleeves. The Green had a lament rising from it, a visible lament, trees lowered into grey, ducks paddling, letting out little cries that got lost in the willow trees.

One stood on Grafton Street, one saw one's life.

Leo and Jeremy left Dublin on the mailboat, pocket money in their jackets, enough to get another boat to France. They'd go south; it was too late to pick grapes now but perhaps they'd get to Crete and get jobs in a cork factory or on an industrial plant on the island.

Young men bearing images of the Guru Maharajii on their badges sat around, their uniform polite.

A busker played with a string and Dublin sat up against the evening light, chimneys, domes; the curtain call of a country where men murdered children, where British army vehicles weighed purposelessly against the night, where prosperity wrestled with poverty, where in one part a woman judged her canvas, a terrible peace in her eyes.